KU-519-782

Joss found it difficult to move for a second as the smile Melissa had just aimed in his direction had been a bright and trusting one which had made her brown eyes sparkle with delight.

Something started stirring deep within him—a feeling he hadn't felt for such a long time. Whatever it was, he didn't want it. He just wanted to do his job, to live his life, and not have to worry about the pain pretty women caused.

She was jostled from behind, and it was a purely protective instinct which made him put his arm around her. He steadied her, but decided to let his arm stay exactly where it was, glad of the excuse to draw her a little closer to him.

'Three!'

'Two!'

She turned to look up at him.

'One!'

His arm tightened, drawing her closer.

'Happy New Year, Lis.'

'Happy New Year, Joss.'

And, with that, he bent his head and brushed his lips across hers.

Lucy Clark is a husband-and-wife writing team. They enjoy taking holidays with their two children, during which they discuss and develop new ideas for their books using the fantastic Australian scenery. They use their daily walks to talk over characterisation and fine details of the wonderful stories they produce, and are avid movie buffs. They live on the edge of a popular wine district in South Australia, and enjoy spending family time together at weekends.

Recent titles by the same author:

BRIDE ON THE CHILDREN'S WARD
SURGEON BOSS, BACHELOR DAD
A MOTHER FOR HIS TWINS
CHILDREN'S DOCTOR, CHRISTMAS BRIDE

NEW BOSS,
NEW-YEAR BRIDE

BY
LUCY CLARK

MILLS & BOON

All the characters in this book have no existence outside
the imagination of the author, and have no relation
whatsoever to anyone bearing the same name or names.
They are not even distantly inspired by any individual
known or unknown to the author, and all the incidents
are pure invention.

All Rights Reserved including the right of reproduction
in whole or in part in any form. This edition is published
by arrangement with Harlequin Enterprises II BV/S.à.r.l.
The text of this publication or any part thereof may
not be reproduced or transmitted in any form or by
any means, electronic or mechanical, including
photocopying, recording, storage in an information
retrieval system, or otherwise, without the written
permission of the publisher.

® and TM are trademarks owned and used by the
trademark owner and/or its licensee. Trademarks marked
with ® are registered with the United Kingdom Patent
Office and/or the Office for Harmonisation in the
Internal Market and in other countries.

First published in Great Britain 2009
Large Print edition 2010
Harlequin Mills & Boon Limited,
Eton House, 18-24 Paradise Road,
Richmond, Surrey TW9 1SR

© Anne Clark and Peter Clark 2009

ISBN: 978 0 263 21099 6

Harlequin Mills & Boon policy is to use papers that are
natural, renewable and recyclable products and made
from wood grown in sustainable forests. The logging and
manufacturing processes conform to the legal environmental
regulations of the country of origin.

Printed and bound in Great Britain
by CPI Antony Rowe, Chippenham, Wiltshire

	BIRMINGHAM LIBRARIES	
	NORTHFIELD LIBRARY	
HJ	28-Jun-2010	
AF ROM	£13.99	

NEW BOSS,
NEW-YEAR BRIDE

To Lisa & Brenton—
who inspired the pigmy blow-gun dart!
Cheers!
Rom 15:1-4

CHAPTER ONE

THIS was it. Melissa Clarkson took a deep breath and looked up at the building which seemed to stand in the middle of nowhere, surrounded by rich ochre dirt.

This was it?

'What a dump,' she mumbled under her breath. How could her brother work in such a place? She frowned, then realised she wasn't here to judge him. She had come to Australia's west to meet her brother—for the first time.

Dex Crawford was the biological brother she'd been told about just over two years ago, and it had taken her quite some time to track him down. Now, today, she was finally going to meet him. He knew she was coming. He knew she was going to be working alongside him for the next twelve months as part of the Didja medical team, providing medical care to the community and the workers at the large industrial mine which was situated not too far out of town. Melissa also knew her brother hadn't been too keen at the prospect of meeting her, and she could understand that. When a complete stranger told you that you were biologically related it was bound to come as a shock.

She'd been travelling for what seemed to be for ever, but after taking a plane from Tasmania to Melbourne, and another plane from Melbourne to Perth—with a quick three-hour stopover in Adelaide along the way—she'd made her way to the 'Outback' train station and boarded just before midnight. She hadn't slept much, whether due to the heavy rocking of the train or to apprehension at the brand-new adventure staring her in the face. Either way, when she'd arrived in Didja hope had mingled with excitement at the thought that Dex might be there to meet her.

The hope had dwindled as she'd slung her carry-on luggage across her shoulder and gathered her two suitcases, never more thankful that they were on wheels. She'd trudged out into the almost noon sun and studied a very old town map in the hope that it would show her the way to the medical clinic.

And now she stood in front of this dilapidated building, excitement at her new adventure being sucked up into the dry heat. 'This can't be it,' she murmured, not wanting to take another step further lest the building fall down right before her very eyes.

'Excuse me?'

Melissa turned at the rich deep tones and shielded her eyes as she looked up and then up some more into the face of the rather tall man who now stood next to her.

'Are you Melissa Clarkson?'

'Yes. Yes, I am.' Hope flared once more. Was this him? Was this tall, handsome stranger her brother? 'Are you Dex?'

'No, I'm Joss,' he corrected, and held out his hand. 'Josiah Lawson.'

'Ah.' Melissa tried not to show her disappointment as she shook his hand. She also tried to ignore the way her hand, which was warmly enveloped within his, felt safe and secure. Perhaps it was because she was so incredibly out of her comfort zone at the moment, and any remote sense of security would be bound to cause her to react to a simple handshake from a handsome stranger. Josiah Lawson was her new boss. The owner of the Didja clinic and the man who had offered her not only a twelve-month contract but the opportunity to take her time and really get to know her brother.

'Were you expecting Dex to pick you up?'

'I was…hoping.' And he was still holding her hand.

Unlike him, she was not wearing sunglasses—nor a hat—and when he looked into her deep brown eyes he could instantly see the family resemblance. The deep red sun-dress she wore high-lighted the fairness of her skin and complemented her blonde hair, which had been swept back into a single ponytail. Joss knew she'd been travelling for well over twenty-four hours, yet somehow she'd managed to look as fresh as a daisy.

It was clear she'd been hoping her biological brother would pick her up, would show an interest in her arriving in town, but he hadn't. Dex didn't seem to care one way or the other about his new 'surprise sister'—as he called her—and it had been Joss who had needed to point out the benefits in at least meeting Melissa. Still, she didn't need to know all of that.

'Dex is in clinic, so I volunteered to come and meet your train.' He smiled politely at her. 'I apologise most profusely for being late, and then, I confess, I couldn't find you.' He gestured to the building in front of them with his free hand. 'What are you doing in this part of town?'

Melissa was a little puzzled at his words. She pointed to the building in front of them. 'Finding the clinic.'

'The clinic? You think this is the clinic?' His lips twitched into a small smile and she wished she could see his eyes, but they were hidden behind dark sunglasses and the bushman's hat planted firmly on his head.

'Isn't it? I read the town map at the train station and it said…' She shook her head and sighed. 'I am relieved, though. How anyone could practise medicine in this old… building—'

'For want of a better word,' he interjected.

'—is beyond me.'

'Well, Dr Clarkson, allow me to escort you to the real Didja clinic.' It was only now that he dropped her hand and in turn picked up both of her suitcases. 'This way, if you please.'

What on earth was he doing? He'd been holding her hand for too long—like a complete moron. She was a colleague. She was here to work and that, as far as he was concerned, was all there was to it. The fact that she was a bit of a looker meant nothing, either.

He led her down the side of the old medical centre, her suitcases proving to be no effort for him whatsoever. Melissa watched as he walked a few steps in front of her, admiring the length of his back, the broadness of his shoulders and the flexed arm muscles which were almost straining to break through his short-sleeved cotton shirt.

He wore thick socks with a pair of well-worn work boots, and a pair of long khaki shorts which provided her with the view of just enough tanned leg covered in dark curly hairs. Very nice, well muscled legs. His butt was firm from what she could see, as the cotton shirt was untucked. Combined with the hat, he looked nothing like a doctor—or at least nothing like the doctors she was used to working with in a pristine hospital setting. She had to keep reminding herself that this was, to all intents and purposes, the Outback of Australia, even though she wasn't in the Northern Territory, or Far North Queensland, where most people equated the Outback to be.

She had landed herself in the inland Western Australian Outback, and judging by the vast contrast with Tasmania's lush greenness she knew she was most definitely a very long way from home.

They'd rounded the old clinic and were walking down what Melissa realised was a small side street, although it appeared to be no more than a clearing in the never-ending dirt. Joss then turned right down an even smaller clearing. A lane, perhaps? Within another minute, Melissa found herself walking through what she belatedly realised was someone's front garden. There were plenty of green gum trees and bright flowering bottle brushes around the house, and the green of the leaves and the brown of the trunks blended in a picturesque way with the ochre ground. There was the odd patch of grass, but it wasn't a vibrant green—rather it was dull and brittle as they walked over the scattered tufts.

'Uh…' She couldn't help feeling uncomfortable. 'Joss?'

'Yes?'

'Are you sure this is the right way?'

He stopped and looked at her, his lips twitching a little. It was on the tip of his tongue to come back with a witty comment, but at the tired, confused look in her eyes he decided she'd probably had enough for the time being, and wanted nothing more than to lie down in a bed beneath a cooling ceiling fan and sleep.

'I'm sure.'

He continued on, seemingly not at all perturbed that he was walking through someone else's garden. They continued on down the side of the house and into the backyard, which boasted even more of the withered grass and native evergreen gum trees, although these trees had been decorated with bright coloured tinsel, reminding Melissa that Christmas had been just a week ago. Why did it seem like months had already passed? The New Year began tomorrow, meaning that when the clock struck midnight the beginning of the next phase of her life would really begin. Her year in Didja, working alongside the man before her and her brand-new brother, would commence.

Her stomach churned at the thought of finally meeting Dex, of coming face to face with him, of being able to touch him. Her little brother… And the moment was drawing closer and closer with each step she took.

Melissa snapped out of her reverie as Joss called a cheery greeting to a woman pegging out washing on the line.

'This is the new doctor at the clinic,' he remarked, putting her suitcases down for a moment so he could perform the introductions.

Melissa had pasted on a smile and was ready to shake hands and be polite. She was most certainly surprised when the woman dropped the pegs and wet clothes back into the basket and flung both arms around Melissa, squealing with delight as she did so.

'Oh, Doc Joss. You said you'd do it. You said you'd do it and you've done it.'

The woman was exuberant as her strong arms kept squeezing Melissa. Melissa stared with wide-eyed astonishment at her new colleague. Joss merely chuckled. Melissa mouthed the words 'help me', but it was a good five seconds later that Joss decided to do just that.

'All right, Minerva. Put her down. Let her go.'

'You did it, Doc Joss. She's here. She's here!' Minerva was now past the point of excitement.

'I take it my arriving in town is a good thing?' Melissa straightened her clothes as she spoke.

'You could say that.' Joss dropped his tone and stepped closer, the spicy scent of whatever he was wearing winding around her with a very pleasing effect. 'I've been trying to get a female doctor to come to Didja for quite some time.'

'Hence why I've been locked into a twelve-month contract?'

'Hence,' he agreed with a smile, and dipped his sunglasses down his nose to look at her.

Melissa tried not to gasp out loud as she stared into the most gorgeous and hypnotic pair of blue eyes she'd ever seen. No wonder he shielded them. Not to protect them from the bright sunlight, but in order to make sure life continued on its merry way—because she was certain that many women could simply sit around all day staring into those gorgeous depths, sighing whilst they did so.

'Oh, Doc Joss. I'm very happy. And you, Doc Melissa. You're here. You've come. Us sheilas—we need you. Honest we do.'

Minerva's bright interjections were enough to force Melissa to look away from her new boss's face. What had she been doing? Staring at her boss? Being highly unprofessional. Minerva was heading towards her again, arms outstretched for another hug, and mentally Melissa braced herself.

'Leave her,' Joss remarked kindly, and placed both hands on Minerva's shoulders, keeping her away from scaring off his new colleague.

'I'm gonna go call everyone. This is a happy day. Happy day,' she repeated as, without a hint of farewell, she turned and went into the house.

In another second they were alone again, and Joss picked up the suitcases, indicating they should continue on their way.

'Well, if this is the reaction you're going to get, I guess it means your clinics are going to be nice and full for quite some time.'

'I guess.' So long as she still had time to get to know her brother, she was fine with her work load. Making friends and being liked by the community were all important, but they weren't her top priority, and Melissa was the type of woman who found it easier by far to keep things in order of priority. Life seemed to work better that way, and it also led to less heartache.

At the bottom of the garden they turned right onto a concrete footpath, and there before her was the main street of the town—Didjabrindagrogalon—known affectionately to its inhabitants as Didja.

'And there's the clinic.' Joss waved his hand with a flourish and Melissa stared at the building. Now, *this* was what she had been expecting. 'We have a little ten-bed hospital out the back, and a small surgery—usually only used for emergencies.'

'And you have nursing staff?'

'Quite a few of the women in town are nurses, or retired nurses who are willing to do a few days here and there. Bub's the only nurse employed full-time. She's in charge of the hospital and rules it with a heart of gold and a rod of iron. You'll like her.'

'I have no doubt.' They headed further down the footpath towards a pedestrian crossing. 'And you're a qualified general surgeon, correct?'

'I am.'

'And Dex is the A&E specialist.'

'He is.'

Melissa nodded, but could feel Joss watching her. 'Something wrong?' she asked.

'No. I'm just wondering whether you're going to voice the questions which I can see running around in your mind.'

'You can see into my mind?' Melissa raised her eyebrows in teasing as he stopped by the kerb. There wasn't a single moving car on the road, but still both of them stood there, waiting and looking at each other.

'I can see that you're wondering what on earth could have brought Dex and I all the way to the middle of nowhere.'

'I assure you I was wondering no such thing. Besides, I can't talk. I'm a qualified OB/GYN, and I know exactly what's brought me to the middle of nowhere, as you term it. Everyone has their own reasons for doing things, Joss. Despite whatever they may be, Didja is a fortunate town to have such highly trained doctors and a group of dedicated nurses working for it.'

Joss frowned slightly as he looked down at her, his shoulders squaring as he took a deep breath, filling his lungs. 'Wow.'

'Wow, what?'

He shook his head. 'It's been a long time since I've heard anyone talk like that.' Joss checked again for cars, but still didn't move. He was impressed with what she'd said because the few locum doctors who had previously come out to Didja had been snobbish and prejudiced against anyone who chose to live in such a place. 'I think you're going to fit in just fine here, Dr Clarkson.'

'Even though my main motive for coming here is so I can get to know my brother?'

'Even though,' he agreed with a slight nod.

Joss watched as a dog rushed by in hot pursuit of a piece of paper floating on the light breeze. He picked up her suitcases and headed across the road. Melissa followed, and the instant she stepped out onto the road, a car came around the corner. She quickened her pace, but thankfully the car was going quite slowly. The driver wound down the window and called to Joss.

'Is that her?'

'Yes,' he returned as he reached the other side of the road.

The driver waved at Melissa. 'I'll be sure to tell the missus you're in town.' With that, he drove off.

Melissa stepped onto the footpath, looking up at Joss. 'I'm beginning to feel like something of a celebrity.'

'You should be, and tonight—in your honour—the whole town will gather to celebrate your arrival.' He pointed to a group of men down the street, who were all working hard setting up a stage. 'There'll be a band, a lot of dancing, some fireworks and a whole lotta Outback fun.'

'In my honour?' she asked sceptically, not believing a word he said.

'Of course.' Joss's lips twitched.

'And not the fact that it's New Year's Eve?'

He shrugged away her words. 'Pure coincidence.' He picked up her suitcases again and headed down the street. 'Best get you out of this sun. Didn't you bring a hat?'

Melissa watched him go, amazed at the way she really liked being in his company. This man, this stranger who was her boss. This man who had founded the clinic here in Didja, who had moved to this Outback land for some reason. Whilst she'd told him she wasn't curious, that hadn't been entirely true. What made a man—a general surgeon—come to the middle of nowhere and set up first-class medical facilities? And it wasn't just Joss she was curious about but her brother as well. What had made Dex come here? Why had he stayed? Why was he so indifferent about meeting her? These were definitely top of the list in the questions department, and she hoped her time here would not only help her discover the answers but also to form some sort of relationship with Dex.

'I'm guessing you'll be wanting to find your room first and get settled in, rather than having a tour of the facilities.'

'It would be nice to shower and change.'

'No doubt.' He headed down a small driveway beside the clinic, and it was then she realised that out at the back of the clinic was another building which looked just like a small block of flats. 'It's not much,' he said, indicating the building with an incline of his head. 'But it's home. There are four apartments here—the end one is currently being used for storage, but we're hoping to have a locum come on a regular basis and that's where he or she will be accommodated.'

'With three doctors here now, do you still need a locum?'

'The mining company has just announced their expansion plans. Another two hundred workers will be in the area by the middle of next year. And we cover a huge area. Three doctors simply won't be enough. If we could get a fourth on a permanent basis that would be fantastic, and if they could specialise in paediatrics it would be even better, but a man can only hope.'

Melissa had been watching him walk again, liking the firmness of his stride. When he stopped outside a door she almost careered into him, she'd been so intent on checking him out. 'Uh…you know,' she said quickly, hoping he hadn't seen her looking so closely at his derierre, 'I might be able to suggest a friend who's a paediatrician. She's been looking for somewhere different to work.'

'Really? Well, I'd certainly be interested to learn more. In the meantime…' He pointed to the door next to them. 'Here's your apartment. Number three. I'm next door in two if you need anything or have any questions.' He set the suitcases down and pulled a set of keys from his pocket. He chose one and unlocked her door. 'I'll get your keys to you.'

'That would be handy—otherwise I'd have to come and find you each time I needed my door unlocked.'

He chuckled at her statement. She was funny. She was relaxed. He only hoped she'd stay for the full twelve months of her contract. He knew she'd come here to find her brother, and he'd exploited the situation to his advantage by providing her with twelve long months to break through Dex's defences. He only hoped the frustration she'd feel due to Dex's indifference to the entire situation wouldn't make her want to flee.

'That wouldn't be good—for either of us. I'll also try and get you an up-to-date map of the town, so you don't end up in places where a dilapidated building could fall down around you.'

'I'd appreciate it.' She went to pick up one of her suitcases but Joss waved her away. He pushed open her door and headed inside, his firm muscles rippling once again as he carried her bags. 'Tell me, Joss. Why do you lock the doors? I thought here in the Outback there was no need?'

'There never used to be. Of course I keep the clinic locked up tighter than Fort Knox, but as a general rule people are fairly relaxed when it comes to security. The town, though, has two full-time police officers.'

'Impressive.'

'Along with the growth of a town comes growth in crime, and unfortunately Didja isn't the sleepy little town it used to be.'

'The mining company changed all that?'

'Not the mining company *per se*, but some of the people they've employed over the years.'

'It happens.'

'It does.'

Melissa hesitated for a second. She'd been looking forward to the opportunity of showering and changing for quite some time, but now she found herself wanting to prolong Joss's little visit. He was a really nice man, and she was happy about that given that she'd be working with him for the next year. Until her arrival they'd only exchanged the odd e-mail after she'd been accepted for the position and signed the contracts, and even those e-mails had mostly been filled with instructions. Now, though, she found herself quite…intrigued by him. She'd spent the last fifteen or so minutes in his company and he'd definitely made an impact.

An impact which increased when he removed his hat and his sunglasses. His hair was dark brown, short, but slightly curling around the collar. It was as though he knew he needed a haircut but couldn't be bothered. And those eyes. Those deep blue eyes which she'd only been given a hint of earlier on were now staring at her as though she was an enigma, a puzzle, and one he wasn't sure he wanted to figure out.

'So this is your apartment.' He turned away, needing to look somewhere else—anywhere other than at the woman who was watching him with such concentrated intent. 'Air-conditioning controls are here. Ceiling fan controls are on the wall by the bed.' He pointed, then shrugged. 'I guess that's the basics covered.'

Melissa smiled. 'You've been a great tour guide so far.'

'Tour guide?' He smiled at the words. 'I guess I have, and you're welcome. You've got some time to have a few hours' rest before the big festivities begin. Clinic—fingers crossed—should finish on time, and then it's all about the party.'

'All about the party?' she repeated.

'The community waits all year for this event. It's big.'

'Looks as though I came on the right day.'

'Looks as though you did.' He took a few steps towards the door.

'So…how do I get to these festivities? I'm presuming they're at the pub or somewhere central?'

'Exactly. Everyone will be quitting work a little earlier today, so basically all you need to do is join the throng of people heading in that direction. The pub's right in the centre of the town. That's the Aussie way of doing things. You build the pub first, and the rest of the town sort of just takes shape around it.'

'Sounds sensible—especially given how hot it is out here.'

'And it'll stay at these temperatures for the next six months. You'll get used to it soon enough. The heat and the flies. A staple of Outback life.'

'Careful. You might make me question my decision to stay.'

'Ahh, you're contracted for a whole twelve months, Dr Clarkson, and I'll not be letting you go so easily.' There was playfulness to his words, but also a hint of underlying seriousness.

'I was just teasing. I'll not be going anywhere. You can rest assured on that point.'

'Good. That's good to hear.'

Again there was a moment of silence as they stood there looking at each other. This time Melissa didn't rush to fill the void, content just to look at him. She must have made him slightly uncomfortable, though, because he took the few remaining steps to her door and opened it, letting a bright beam of sunlight into the room. He looked good, standing there, his body half outlined by the light, all golden and shiny.

'I'll leave you to it.'

'Yes. Thanks again. Much appreciated—you know, rescuing me from old buildings and the like.'

'You're welcome, Melissa.'

'Lis,' she ventured. 'My friends call me Lis.'

'Lis.' He smiled down at her, pleased that she was opening up. This was a small and intimate community and there were no grounds for pomp and ceremony. 'Listen, just to make sure you find your way about town and don't run the risk of getting trampled by a throng of thirsty miners, why don't I meet you here at around half past five?'

The instant the words were out of his mouth he

regretted them. Why had he offered to do that? She was his colleague. The town wasn't that big. She'd find her own way. Still, perhaps this was him being friendly. He raised his eyebrows at the thought. He hadn't been friendly to a stranger in…he wasn't sure how long.

She nodded, pleased she wouldn't have to take her first steps into town life by herself. 'Sounds good.'

'OK. I guess I'll see you then.' He shoved his hands into the pockets of his shorts and took a half a step backwards. 'I need to check on how many patients are left. Enjoy the break of not working, because from tomorrow, public holiday or not, you'll be seeing patients.'

'Starting me off in the manner in which you want me to continue?'

He chuckled. 'Something like that. Remember, just sing out if you need any help or have any questions. Everyone's very friendly and willing to help you settle in with as little fuss as possible.'

So she was beginning to realise—and also, she thought as she closed the door after he'd left, how great it was that her professional and personal lives had managed to interconnect so seamlessly for once. She wanted to spend time getting to know her biological brother, and the Didja clinic needed an OB/GYN. It was a win-win. At least, she hoped it was.

As Melissa shut the door after him Joss headed back to the clinic, his thoughts on his new employee. She was very pretty, and he hoped that didn't cause too much of a stir within the community. Whilst forty percent of the miners were married, sixty percent weren't, and that didn't include a lot of the other young men who lived in the town but didn't work for the mining company.

Ordinarily Dex—who had been voted bachelor of the year for the last two years running—would have been his biggest concern, but given the family connection Joss could strike him off the list.

He nodded to himself, pleased Melissa had accepted his invitation for this evening. He was determined not only to escort her to the celebration this evening but to make sure she returned safely to her apartment—alone. It had been difficult enough trying to get a female doctor to come and live here for more than a month. He wasn't going to have one of the miners take her focus away from her work.

And there was no reason for him to be concerned about himself, because one of his main motivations for settling in Didja in the first place was to get away from women. No. His pretty colleague was just that. She was pretty and she was a colleague. Enough said.

At five-thirty Melissa was ready. More than ready, in fact. She'd had enough time to shower and refresh herself, but after that she hadn't felt at all sleepy and so had walked the short block to where the hub of Didja existed—the pub.

She hadn't felt comfortable going inside, but had instead found a store where she could purchase a sun-hat, some sun-screen and a pair of sun-glasses—given that hers had broken on the train journey here. She'd also bought some groceries, adding to her pile the important insect repellent and fly swat. In Tasmania the flies only came out on hot days, and as those were few and far between she wasn't at all used to the constant need to swat in front of her face and around her body.

She'd returned to her apartment, unpacked,

found a home for everything and managed to get a full hour's sleep before getting ready. She'd chosen a simple sun-dress in a pale pink colour she'd bought on impulse two days before she'd left Tasmania. She liked being on time, punctual whenever possible, which sometimes with clinics and a surgical list wasn't always possible. Still, she'd been checking the peephole through her door on a regular basis for the past ten minutes, just in case Joss had been running early. As the clock ticked towards twenty minutes to six, she realised he was actually running late.

Sighing, she decided to put the kettle on and have a soothing cup of tea. No sooner had she filled the kettle than the knock came at her door. Melissa abandoned her relaxation efforts, picked up her hat and opened the door. There he was. Her new boss. Dressed in freshly laundered shorts and cotton short-sleeve shirt, his blue eyes twinkling happily, he stood before her looking— really silly.

'What…?' A laugh bubbled up as she shook her head. 'What *are* you wearing?'

Joss flicked at a cork that swung around from the hat on his head. 'What? This old thing?' He shrugged and moved his head slightly from side to side. The little corks which were dangling down on strings from his bush hat jangled around. 'I wear it every New Year's Eve.'

'You do? What on earth for?' She came out of her apartment and shut the door behind her, placing her new hat firmly on her head. Although it was getting on for six o'clock, due to daylight saving the sun wouldn't go down for at least another three hours, and it was still rather sticky and very warm.

'To remind me not to make any New Year's resolutions.'

'You don't believe in them?' They started walking down the street and Melissa was surprised to see so many people out and about. For a sleepy little Outback town it looked as if they were sure about to have one major humdinger of a party.

'Not really. I just don't see why people only think they can change at New Year. Anyone can change at any time in their life. You don't need to wait for a change in the calendar to make a difference to your life—especially if it's a difference that's going to make you happier.'

'Good point. But I'm still not getting the hat.'

Joss chuckled. 'The hat—due to the pure silliness of it—reminds me that New Year's resolutions are just as silly.'

'For you?'

'Yes. For me. Sorry. I guess I sound all judgemental and the like. Perhaps some people need the push of a New Year to help them to change.'

'Perhaps they do.'

Joss glanced at her through the swinging corks. 'Have you already made your resolution? Is coming here to Didja your change?'

'It is.'

'To get to know your brother?'

'Yes.'

'But you didn't wait until the New Year arrived to make the decision?'

'No.'

'With or without the changing of the calendar you still would have pursued Dex. Am I right?'

'You are.'

'So you're the same as me, then. A person of action. A person who sets themselves a goal, then figures out the best route to get there.'

'I guess.' Melissa pondered on his words for a

moment. 'Although sometimes the way I choose to go doesn't always come about.'

'Sounds as though there's a story there. Bad relationship?'

'Everyone has one.' She shrugged. It was true that she liked her new boss, liked him a great deal in fact, but he was also a stranger—and telling a stranger of her broken engagement wasn't something she was about to do.

'Yes, they do. But tonight—tonight is for celebrating. To say goodbye to the old and hello to the new.'

'Yes.'

'You are going to meet so many people tonight and no doubt remember next to none of them.'

'Yes,' she repeated, with absolute gusto.

'It's going to be a great night, ending with some brilliant fireworks.'

'Fireworks? Really?'

'Well…' Joss shrugged. 'Nev and Kev are setting them up, so goodness knows what will eventuate.'

'Let's hope it's not a long night in Theatre.'

'My sentiments exactly.' Joss smiled down at her. 'Do you know something, Dr Clarkson?'

'What, Dr Lawson?'

'I think you're going to fit into Didja quite nicely.'

'It's kind of you to say so.' And she hoped he was right. The only thing was she hadn't yet met Dex, and goodness only knew how he'd take to having a big sister in town—a big sister he seemed less then keen to meet.

As the evening progressed, Melissa was indeed introduced to all and sundry. She gave up trying to remember names, except those of the nurses and other clinical staff Joss introduced her to. He played the polite host and stuck by her side the entire time, and she was grateful to be able to use him as a sort of anchor for her first night in town.

Finally, though, the moment she'd been both waiting for and silently dreading arrived, and it was once again Joss who performed the introductions.

'Melissa. This is Dex.'

Melissa smiled brightly up at the man who had almost reluctantly sauntered over to them. Her heart was pounding with excitement and trepidation. Here he was. Her brother. Standing before her. For two years she'd been searching for him and now here he was. It wasn't exactly the TV show reunion she'd been hoping for, but it didn't really matter any more. They were now in the same place at the same time. The brother she'd never had the chance to know. Tears pricked behind her eyes but she pushed them away.

'Welcome to Didja.' Dex's words were deep, his tone polite, and she realised it was just as if he was greeting a normal colleague.

Melissa looked him up and down, searching unconsciously for some sort of resemblance. It appeared that he was doing the same as they stood there, just staring at each other. He had brown hair, a bit longer than Joss's, and he had brown eyes. Brown eyes which were the exact same shade and shape as her own. His nose wasn't straight, indicating a break at some point, and his lips weren't smiling at all.

Joss watched them both, picking up on the similarities and dismissing any doubt he might have had about Melissa's claims. He could tell Dex was nervous, but it was something only he would pick up on because they'd known each other for so long. This was a big moment for his friend, and he was glad he could be there to support him.

'So you're my sister?' Dex finally broke the silence.

'Yes.' Melissa swallowed over the lump in her throat.

'My real sister?'

'Yes.'

'Fair enough.' He raised a glass bottle of light beer to his lips and took a swig. 'Enjoy the party.' He took a few steps away and then turned back. 'Oh, and Happy New Year. Hope it's a good one for ya.'

'Thanks. And for you, too.'

He shrugged, then was swallowed up by the throng of people. Melissa closed her eyes, trying to control the rising mix of emotions which were surging through her. Confusion, disappointment, anxiety, frustration, elation. They were all jumbling around together.

When she opened her eyes, she found Joss watching her very closely.

'You all right?'

'Yes.' She let go of the breath she hadn't realised she'd been holding. 'Yes, I'm fine.

Thank you.' She pursed her lips and gazed out into the crowd standing around in the street, most of them with a drink in hand, the pub doing a roaring trade. 'I don't know what I was expecting, but…' She shook her head. 'That wasn't it.'

'He's a very private man.'

'He seems very…personable.' She caught a glimpse of him laughing raucously with a bunch of mates.

'He is, but the real Dex is locked up deep inside. You're a potential threat to that. Still, he admires you for having the guts to come.'

Hope flared in Melissa's eyes as she looked up at Joss. 'He said that?'

'Not in so many words, but I can read it in him.'

'How long have you known him?'

Joss thought for a moment. 'Well over a decade. We've been friends since medical school.'

'Then you're the perfect person.'

He eyed her sceptically. 'The perfect person for what?' But it was too late. He already knew what she was about to say.

'The perfect person to help me to get to know him.' With that, she finished the glass of refreshing ginger ale she'd been holding and smiled up at him. 'Now, are we going to mingle some more? I'm sure there are at least another hundred people simply dying to meet me.'

Joss found it difficult to move for a second, as the smile she'd just aimed in his direction had been a bright and trusting one which had made her brown eyes sparkle with delight. Her whole being radiated instant happiness. Something stirred deep within him—a feeling he hadn't felt for such a long time. Admiration? Attraction? Whatever it was, he didn't want it. He just wanted to do his job, to live his life, and not have to worry about the pain and consternation pretty women caused.

Still, he played the host and stayed by her side, watching the relaxed and friendly way she was with everyone they met. As he'd predicted, the men in the town most certainly appreciated the new doctor, but where he saw leering grins and ulterior motives Melissa saw only Outback hospitality and friendliness.

When the time came for the big countdown there were quite a few men standing close to her, getting ready to swoop down and kiss her as midnight arrived. She was jostled from behind, and it was purely a protective instinct which made him put his arm around her. He steadied her and decided to let his arm stay exactly where it was, glad of the excuse to draw her a little closer to him, away from the men around them.

'Get ready everyone,' the Mayor called from the small podium which had been hastily erected in the centre of the only crossroad in town. There was an enormous crowd, and they were all packed in like sheep around the stage. 'It's time for the final countdown.'

'Ten!'

'Nine!'

'Eight!'

Melissa was pushed again from behind, and felt Joss's arm tighten around her. She couldn't help the tingles which spread through her body at his touch. Was he protecting her from the other men crowded around them? Or was he displaying an interest which was more than friendship for his new colleague? She wasn't at all sure, but decided the easiest thing she could do was to do nothing.

What she did know was that, whatever cologne Joss wore, the spicy, heady scent was driving her to distraction. The warmth of his arm against her skin almost burned through her sun-dress, and as the countdown got lower she found her mouth going dry.

'Three!'

It was getting closer. Melissa parted her lips, the pent-up air escaping. No man had kissed her since Renulf, and whilst she knew this kiss wouldn't really be real, in that it wouldn't mean anything, she was still a little over-awed at the prospect of a total stranger kissing her. It was also very exciting.

'Two!'

She licked her lips and turned to look up at him.

'One!'

His arm tightened, drawing her closer.

'Happy New Year!' everyone yelled, and Joss looked down into her upturned face. It was only then she realised that, thankfully, he'd removed the ridiculous corked hat.

'Happy New Year, Lis.'

'Happy New Year, Joss.'

And, with that, he bent his head and brushed his lips across hers.

CHAPTER TWO

SHOCK.

It was the first emotion he felt. Shock. The way the touch of his mouth against hers, even though it was the most whisperish of kisses, made his body tense with the excited need for more.

Simple.

This wasn't supposed to be a complicated moment. It was New Year and he was fulfilling the tradition to kiss the woman nearest to him as a token of celebration. The fact that he'd made sure *Melissa* was the woman nearest to him was purely for the sake of the clinic. Now, though, now that his mouth was on hers, the innocent pressure increasing to something signifying more than innocence, Joss wondered at the deeper psychology of his actions.

He edged away, allowing the smallest breath

of air to flow between them. He stared at her, unsure of what had just happened.

Melissa had never in all her years been kissed with such delicacy. It was supposed to be a simple New Year's kiss, and as the countdown had fallen she'd looked at the strangers around her and been ever so grateful when Joss had slipped his arm about her waist.

Then, when she'd looked up at him, the world around her had melted away. The throng of people had become non-existent as she'd waited with mounting apprehension for his lips to be pressed to hers. Now that they had she couldn't believe the way her heart was pounding double time against her chest. Nor the way her stomach seemed to be flip-flopping with delight. Or the way her knees had turned to jelly, causing her to lean into him some more. The hard, solid muscle of his chest pressed up against her, filling her with overwhelming warmth and excitement.

They were jostled again from behind, and Melissa stared up at Joss as he stared down at her. Both of them were looking at each other with wide-eyed shock and surprise. What was meant to be a brief peck of a New Year's kiss had turned

into something more…something untapped…
something sensual.

Fireworks were bursting high above them,
spreading their colour, sound and smell far and
wide in the cloudless night sky. As the loud
bang from the explosions reverberated around
them she felt as though her own set of fireworks
were going off inside her. Honestly, what had
just happened?

'Right. Now, move over, Doc,' a bloke said
from just behind Joss. 'It's my turn.'

'And then me,' another said.

'I'm next in line,' chorused yet another.

Joss broke his gaze from Melissa's to turn and
look at the men in question. 'This isn't a kissing
booth,' he joked as he took a step away from her,
needing some distance. 'You've gotta wait for
the Australia Day Fair for that to happen.' It was
a throwaway line, and said in complete jest, but
that wasn't the way it was taken.

'The new sheila doc's doing a kissing booth at
the Fair?' one of them asked.

'Whoo-ee!' The other clapped his hands
together. 'I'll be looking forward to that.'

'No. That's not what I mea—' Joss tried, but it

was too late. Word was spreading like wildfire, and he looked down at Melissa and shrugged.

'There's a kissing booth at the Australia Day Fair?' she asked, a little perplexed at this town's idiosyncrasies. 'Bit outdated, isn't it?'

Joss crossed his arms over his chest. 'Outdated, eh? What would you suggest in order to bring Didja into the present century? A booth where you can dunk someone in water?'

'Well, why not? It's still fun.'

'Would you be willing to be dunked?'

'Better than a kissing booth,' she murmured, trying not to speak too loud in case she offended any of the men surrounding her. 'And by outdated I meant that in this day and age, with knowledge about communicable diseases and the like…'

'So you're telling me you've just given me a disease?'

'That's not what I meant.' Melissa sighed, feeling completely exasperated. What had happened in the last few seconds? One moment Joss had been kissing her, and now he seemed to be teasing her. She just didn't understand.

She hadn't come here to become romantically involved with anyone. In fact, it was the last thing on her mind. One failed engagement was enough for her, and when Renulf had ended the engagement she'd once more been left all alone. Scared and alone. It had seemed to be the way her life was destined to be…until Dex had agreed to meet her. Therefore romantic entanglements were way, way down on her list of priorities.

So where did that delicious kiss from Joss fit into her new world? He was her colleague, her new boss and her neighbour. He was Dex's best friend. She shook her head, unable to believe she'd allowed herself to lose her head for a moment. She would forget it had ever happened. That was what she'd do. Joss certainly seemed unaffected by it. And yet…the feel of his mouth brushing across hers was still so very real, so very new, and her heart was still racing from…

'Hello, darl. This must be the newest addition to our family.'

Melissa's attention was wrenched away from her confusing thoughts about Joss as she was enveloped in a warm hug from a woman just a little shorter than her.

'Welcome, darl. I'm Bub.'

'Oh. The nurse from the hospital.'

Bub smiled at her. 'Glad to see Josiah has covered all the important particulars. That and making sure you had someone to kiss at midnight.' Bub chuckled as she spoke.

Good Lord. Had the whole town seen their kiss? Inside Melissa was mortified—not because Joss had kissed her, but because she'd allowed him to. Two seconds in this town and she'd completely lost all her common sense.

Deciding it was best not to say anything at all, Melissa merely smiled politely and glanced at Joss. He was raking both hands through his hair, which only made him look more gorgeous with the way it spiked out at different angles. She looked back at Bub, wanting to move away from the subject of the kiss, which was still causing havoc within her body.

'I hear you rule the hospital with a heart of gold and a rod of iron?'

Bub laughed loudly. 'Sounds like something my Josiah would say. Honestly, though, between him and Dex I *have* to rule it with a rod of iron. Two boys, playing around in a big world and having fun. That's not what medicine is all about. It's serious business.' Although Bub's words were spoken sternly, Melissa could see the twinkle in her eyes as she looked up at Joss.

'Agreed.'

'It's going to be nice having another sheila around full-time.' Bub hugged Melissa close again. 'Welcome to Didja, darl, and don't you ever think of leaving.'

'Oh.' Melissa wasn't sure what to say to that. She hadn't actually thought about what she'd do once the contract was over. 'I'll…uh…'

'What am I saying?' Bub tapped her forehead absent-mindedly. 'Of course you're not going to leave—not when your brother's here.' She looked around. 'Speaking of which—where is Dex? I thought he would have been over here with you to see in the New Year. It's a new start for you two. Happy families.'

'I hope so.' Melissa's words were spoken softly. Dex hadn't minded her coming to Didja, but neither had he been enthused. His reception tonight had only confirmed that. But Melissa was a woman on a mission—a mission to get to know her brother. He was all she had left and she had a whole year to make it work.

'Dex?' Joss, who towered above both women,

looked around the crowd. He needed some space between himself and Melissa, and finding Dex might be just the diversion he was looking for. 'I think I saw him go back into the pub.'

'Sounds like Dex. He likes being surrounded by people. Well…girls mainly—but still, as he's such a good-looking bloke, it seems only natural.' Bub looked at Melissa. 'You've met him, right?'

'Joss introduced us,' Melissa agreed, but it was difficult to hide the hint of disappointment she'd felt at Dex's reception.

'He'll come around.' Bub patted her arm, clearly picking up on the undertones. 'Give him time. Dex's the type of man who takes for ever and a day to process information. Having a sister he knows nothing about turn up in town—well, it's bound to shake a man and make him really take a good look at his life. Everything will work out fine. I have a good feeling about it.'

'Thank you, Bub. It's kind of you to say so.' Melissa had taken an instant liking to the woman before her, and was pleased she seemed to have at least one ally. Was Joss an ally, too? She wasn't sure at this stage.

'Good girl.' Bub looked up at Joss. 'Now, as you're still protecting Melissa from the throng of would-be sloppy kissers—which, I must say, was a very good idea on your part—why not take her into the pub and get her another drink? This is a brand-new day of a brand-new year.' Bub looked pointedly from one to the other. 'Anything can happen.'

As they entered the pub, which was chock-full of people, a chorus of 'Happy New Year!' went up and more glasses were clinked in celebration. The publicans behind the bar were working hard, but still enjoying themselves in the festivities.

'Looks as though it's going to be an interesting night,' Joss said close to her ear. She could feel him standing behind her, the warmth from his body surrounding her. 'Let's see if we can't score a couple of chairs and possibly a table.'

'Hey! Doc! Over here,' someone called, and Joss placed his hand in the small of Melissa's back and urged her in the direction of Nev and Kev, two men in their early twenties.

'Happy New Year!' both men chorused.

'Happy New Year!' the crowd roared again.

'Happy New Year,' Joss and Melissa replied,

more sedately. Joss made the introductions and Nev quickly stood to offer his chair to Melissa.

'Thank you.'

'Anything for you.' The young man looked at her as though she'd just hung the moon. It was an odd sensation to be such a superstar in a town where you didn't know anyone. 'I hear you're doing a kissing booth at the Aussie Day Fair?'

Melissa turned to glare at Joss, who merely grinned. 'Actually, I'm not,' she told Nev. 'Sorry.'

'Oh.' He looked so disappointed Melissa almost thought about feeling bad. She shook her head as though to clear it. This was a new year and she wasn't going to be a people-pleaser any more, just to keep the peace. She started chatting with Nev and Kev, asking them to tell her more about the town.

Joss listened and watched the way she interacted with them. He wasn't at all sure what was wrong with him. He sat there in a crowded pub, aware of no one else but the woman beside him. Mesmerising. That was what she was. Mesmerising Melissa. He still couldn't believe he'd kissed her. It was New Year's Eve. It was supposed to be an innocent little kiss.

She had a nice smooth voice, sweet and sultry. The desire to lean over and press another delightful kiss to those lips was almost irresistible. To think of her doing a kissing booth… To think of other men wanting to sample that perfect mouth of hers… A powerful, protective need surged through him and he was astonished by the ferocity of it.

He needed room. Air. Anything. He stood up too quickly, accidentally knocking his chair to the ground. A few people turned to look; others just cheered and called 'Happy New Year' again. Nev, Kev and Melissa were all looking up at him with surprise.

'Just going to go get a drink.' He righted his chair. 'Ahh…Melissa? What can I get for you?'

'The line-up at the bar's a mile long,' Kev told him.

'That's OK.' He needed distance between himself and his new colleague. 'I don't mind.'

'Ginger ale would be fine,' she told him, when he looked at her again. He really did have the most piercing and gorgeous blue eyes. She had the feeling she could simply look into them all day long and do nothing else but sigh. At that thought, she quickly turned her head. 'Uh… thank you,' she added.

'Right.' He took drink orders from Nev and Kev before disappearing.

'So…you're Doc Dex's sister, eh?'

'That's right.'

'The one he didn't know he had?'

'That's right,' she answered again, forcing a smile.

'We should get him over here. Best you two start to get to know each other, eh?'

Before Melissa could say a word Nev was calling Dex's name, even though no one seemed to know where Dex was.

Joss stood in line at the bar and watched Melissa closely. At least with a bit of distance between them he felt a little safer. The woman had incredible brown eyes, soft skin, silky hair and a gorgeous mouth. He closed his eyes, blocking the image of her from sight.

Who was she? She'd burst into his life a few short hours ago and ever since he'd been hard pressed to stop thinking about her. She intrigued him no end, and no woman had intrigued him this much since Christina. That in itself should be evidence enough for him to keep as far, far away from Melissa Clarkson as possible.

'Dude? You OK?'

Joss opened his eyes and looked directly at Dex. 'What are you doing here? You should go and talk to Melissa.'

Dex shrugged. 'Maybe later.'

'She's here, Dex. She's come to Didja to get to know you.'

'I thought she'd come to be our OB/GYN for a year.'

'You don't think she can do both?'

Dex shrugged again. 'I don't know.' Both of them turned to look at her. 'She looks like me. I hadn't expected that.'

'There's no real question that she is your sister. The family genes are strong,' Joss agreed.

'What's she drinking?' Dex wanted to know.

'Ginger ale. Remind you of anyone?'

Dex turned and stared at his friend. 'You're having me on?'

'Nope. She wants ginger ale. Just. Like. You.' He patted his friend on the back. 'Face it, bro. She's your sister, and I think you'll have more in common than you planned on.'

'This is too much.'

'Go talk to her. Just for a few minutes. Say more than hi. She's nice.'

'Yeah.' Dex grinned widely. 'I saw at midnight just how "nice" you thought she was.'

Joss looked down at his feet for a moment before meeting his best friend's teasing gaze. 'Hmm.'

'Yeah, *bro*. You're interested in our new doctor in more than a professional capacity.'

'Untrue.' They shuffled forward in the line. 'The clinic comes first. You know that.'

Mentally, though, he told himself he wanted to find out more about Melissa Clarkson. Did she have a hidden agenda? Did she plan on making half the men in town fall in love with her? What game was she playing? In his experience women always played games, using their wiles to get what they wanted. He'd fallen victim to it once before and he'd paid the price. Since then he'd been overly cautious, and as his new colleague was beginning to arouse feelings in him he hadn't asked for, he was right to be on guard.

Melissa glanced over at where Joss still stood in line at the bar and saw he was talking to Dex.

She shifted in her chair, her feminine intuition telling her that she was no doubt top of their discussion list. She wasn't at all sure she liked it, but there really wasn't much she could do about it.

'Oi! Doc!' A man beside her spoke and leaned down on the table. 'I hear you're going to be doing a kissin' booth at the Fair.'

Melissa moaned and shook her head. Well, Joss had told her that news travelled fast in this one-pub town.

'Go away, Bluey,' Nev said.

'Leave the doc alone,' Kev championed. Thankfully, Bluey did as they suggested and left, but Melissa was starting to wonder what she'd got herself into by coming to the Outback to find her brother. Was she ready for this intimate small-town life? This close-knit community? The way Joss made her feel all gooey inside when he looked down into her eyes?

Melissa looked over to where he was at the bar and found that he was looking back at her. She didn't turn away. She should have, but she just couldn't. It was the classic cliché. Their eyes met across the crowded room.

She stared at him, at those intense blue eyes

which were solely focused on her even though there was a rowdy pub full of people between them. Everything, everyone around them, seemed to stand still, to melt into oblivion.

What on earth *was* this? Melissa's mind was far from working properly, yet the undercurrents which were passing between them were so incredibly real, and when he looked at her as he was now she had the strangest sensation that her life really was about to change. How? She had no idea, but Bub's words that it was a brand-new day and a brand-new year meant that anything could happen.

'Whaddya want, Joss?' asked Wazza, one of the bartenders, and Joss quickly snapped his head around—so fast he almost cracked his neck. Joss gave the order and glanced surreptitiously at Melissa. She was back to chatting with Nev and Kev.

'Yeah!' Dex laughed and clapped him on the back. 'You're not interested in her at all.' The tone was one of pure sarcasm, but Joss decided it was simply better to let it go—because to deny it might also be a lie.

By the time he'd returned to the table and

handed out the drinks he felt more in control of his faculties.

'Great job on the fireworks, mates,' he said to Nev and Kev. 'They went off a real treat, and no casualties this year. Well done.'

Nev preened under Joss's words. 'Thanks, Doc. Yeah, me and Kev really did it—and no burns.'

'Always a bonus,' Joss agreed.

Kev held his glass up and spoke loudly. 'Happy New Year!'

'Happy New Year!' came the resounding reply yet again.

Joss picked up his glass and clinked it with Melissa's. 'To a brand-new day,' he said.

'And a brand-new year,' she agreed, clinking her glass with his. She sipped her ginger ale, ignoring the effect his nearness was having on her equilibrium.

They were joined by a few other people—all interested, it seemed, in her. She guessed that was what happened when you were the new girl in a town where everyone knew everyone else. It was a very busy night, and there were so many people in the pub—most of them standing in line at the bar. Still Melissa found herself scanning the crowds for Dex. She wanted to wish him a Happy New Year, hoping that it would be just that for both of them—that he'd develop the sudden urge not only to get to know her but also to find out about his biological parents. She had all the documentation and lots of photographs to show him, to discuss with him, but she was also a realist and knew he didn't care one way or the other about his biological link.

Joss leaned closer and pointed through the crowd. 'He's over there,' he said softly, his breath fanning her neck. 'Wowing yet another group of women.'

'Who?'

'Dex. You were looking for him, right?'

Melissa turned and looked at the man beside her, only realising belatedly just how close he was to her. If she shifted in her chair a little to the left their lips would once again meet. The thought of that was enough to distract her from her task of looking for her brother. Kissing Joss. Her gaze dropped to his mouth at the same time that her lips parted. Kissing Joss. She met his eyes again and swallowed over the sudden dryness in her throat.

This was nuts—and totally and utterly wrong. He was her boss! They were colleagues. Not to mention neighbours in a very small town. She didn't want anything like this to happen. Not now. Her brain worked overtime to remember the last thing he'd said to her. Dex. Her brother. Yes. She'd been looking for him in the throng of people celebrating the New Year.

'Yes. Thanks. I *was* looking for him.' And now that Joss had pointed him out she should turn and look the other way. But she didn't.

Joss eased back, making the decision and taking action to put some much needed distance between them.

She managed to turn her head and watch her brother, who was talking animatedly to two blondes and a redhead. 'What's he like?'

'Dex?' It was Nev who spoke. 'Sheesh. Don't you even *know*?'

'That's why she's here, remember?' Joss pointed out.

'Oh, yeah. Right. Well, Doc Dex is a real smooth talker.'

'Yeah,' Nev agreed. 'Knows how to charm the ladies.'

'Yeah.' Kev nodded. 'Wish he'd leave some for the rest of us blokes in town.'

'Besides, what's wrong with Doc Joss, eh?' Nev pointed out, and Melissa couldn't help but smile at the mortification which momentarily crossed Joss's face before he hid it.

'Hey, fellas. As much as I appreciate the gesture, I'm not in need of any fixing up in the romance department. Dr Clarkson is here to work, and as far as I'm concerned that is it. She's a valuable member of the clinic team and we don't want to do anything to scare her away.'

Kev snorted. 'Then you'd best squash that rumour that she's gonna be doing a kissing booth at the Fair, otherwise someone's gonna give her a huge smackeroo and she'll be leaving town with a miner before you know it.'

'Uh...actually...' Melissa tried to interject.

'Although if she really *wants* to do a kissing booth,' Nev said, 'we don't want you to stop her.' He smiled and waggled his eyebrows up and down.

Melissa turned worried eyes to Joss.

'I'll fix it, and I'll fix it right now.' And with that Joss stood up and called for everyone's attention. It took a few minutes, but soon everyone was quiet. 'Thank you,' Joss said loudly. 'I'd just like to say a few words. Firstly, allow me to introduce our new doctor—Melissa Clarkson—'

He got no further as a rousing round of applause broke out and someone yelled, 'Here's to the new doc!' Glasses were clinked yet again.

'Here's to kissing booths!' someone else yelled, and an even louder ruckus went up.

Melissa could only close her eyes and hope all this was a bad dream. Well…not *all* of it, but this part at least.

'I have more to say,' Joss called, and again waited for silence. 'Right. Well, I'd like to clear up a rumour that's been spreading like a bad rash. Dr Clarkson will *not*—I repeat, will *not*—be doing a kissing booth at the Australia Day Fair.'

A rousing noise went up again, but this time it was full of booing and hissing and calls of, 'What?' and 'Not fair!'

'And—' Joss called. 'And—Happy New Year.'

'Happy New Year!' went up the cheer, and good moods were instantly restored.

'Satisfied?' Joss sat down and turned to look at a blushing and perplexed Melissa. 'Problem solved.'

'Wow. So that's it? No megaphone? No need to take an ad out in the *Didja Gazette*?'

Joss couldn't help but smile at her words. 'Well…at least everyone now knows. You may still get some offers here and there, but…' He shrugged. 'It's up to you what you do with them.'

Melissa stared at him for a second, but then realised he was teasing her again. She wasn't at all sure what to do. She wasn't at all sure what she'd got herself into. There was only one thing she *could* do. She threw back her head and laughed.

'You're all completely insane,' she said between giggles.

'Welcome to the club,' Joss replied, trying desperately not to let the sound of her laughter affect him. But it was to no avail. The woman was beautiful, smart, and she shared the same sense of humour as him. A dangerous combination, and one he might need to really work on resisting.

A loud noise from the corner snapped his attention back to the other people in the room. 'Oh, no. Not tonight,' he groaned as his gaze followed a line to the disturbance.

'Problem?' Melissa asked.

'Carto and Bluey.'

'Pardon?'

Joss stood from his chair and pointed. Melissa could just make out two men on the opposite side of the pub starting to push and shove each other around. Some of their mates tried to keep them apart, but tempers were starting to flare and a few punches had already been thrown.

Joss started making his way to the bar, and Melissa decided to go with him, making sure she stayed right behind him. She searched the room for Dex and saw that he, too, was working his way over to where the two men were fighting.

'Waz,' Joss said to the bartender. 'Kit.' He need not have said anything. Wazza was already pulling a large first-aid kit from behind the bar.

'That's enough, mates. Leave it alone,' Melissa heard a man call, and looked over to see that Dex had placed himself between the two men, a firm hand on each man's chest. Carto and Bluey were still hurling insults at each other, and just as Joss and Melissa reached the area Bluey leaned forward and swung another punch at Carto. But it missed and connected with Dex's jaw instead.

'Dex!' Melissa couldn't help the rush of

familial concern and rushed to his side. Bluey and Carto, now free of restraint, started laying into each other with abandon, kicking over a table, knocking down other innocent bystanders and generally causing havoc.

Melissa had to fight her way through the throng of women crowding around Dex, all of them panicking. She'd just knelt down beside him when an almighty, piercing whistle cut through the air, followed by a loud, 'Oi! That's enough!'

Melissa looked around to see Joss standing near the two men, arms akimbo, as they both looked sheepishly up at him like naughty schoolboys.

'Bluey—your lip is split. Carto—you're bleeding from your eye. Now, both of you sit down before I knock you into the middle of next week. This is the New Year. You're supposed to change. To grow. To stop fighting in the bar like you do every other week. Just as well your boss has already gone home, or you'd both find your-selves on suspension tomorrow. As it is, I'll have to file a medical report.'

'Aw, come on now, Doc,' Carto protested. 'Do ya have to?' He was hauling himself up off the floor and righting a chair before he sat down.

Someone else righted the table, and people started clearing up the mess which had been made.

'We was only fighting about football.'

'You two are *always* fighting about football. It's not good enough and I've heard it all before. Add to everything, you've knocked Dex off his feet.'

Both men stared over to where Melissa was kneeling beside a dazed Dex.

'Aww, jeepers, Doc. We didn't mean to,' Bluey mumbled as he held a napkin to his lip.

'I don't want to hear it.' Joss looked at Melissa and spoke more calmly. 'How is he?'

'I'm fine.' Dex winced. 'I can't believe I didn't duck in time. So stupid.'

'Stupid was getting in the middle of them in the first place. What were you thinking?' she scolded, sounding to her own ears very much like a big sister.

'Careful there, big sis. You're starting to sound more like my mother.'

'If the shoe fits…' She shrugged and accepted the towel full of ice someone handed to her. 'Hold this.'

'Am I still in the pub?'

'Lying on the floor.'

'Everybody looking?'

'Yeah.'

'Oh, this is going to be so shaming,' he moaned, and tried to move.

She put a hand on him to stop him. 'Stay still.' She held up her finger and got him to track it. 'Good. You seem fine.'

'Except for the totally humiliated part,' he agreed, and she smiled. 'Look—I'm fine, Melissa.' His tone was quiet, yet serious. 'I've been knocked out on many occasions before.'

'It's true,' Joss said from behind her. 'Let's get you to your feet.'

'He's up!' someone yelled, and a rousing cheer met their ears. Several girls started to crowd around Dex, all highly concerned for his wellbeing.

'Happy New Year!' someone else yelled, and once again the night's festivities continued.

'So…' Joss turned Melissa and took a coin from his pocket. 'What do you want? Tails—split lip— or heads—bleeding eye?'

'What?' She looked at him as though he'd grown another head.

'Choose,' Joss urged. 'Heads or tails?'

'Er…tails.'

Joss spun the coin into the air before neatly catching it and placing it on the top of his hand. He held the coin out for her to see. 'Tails it is.'

'All right!' Bluey punched the air. 'I get the sheila doc.'

'Is this the way you make *all* important medical decisions?' Melissa asked as she pulled on a pair of gloves from the medical kit.

Joss merely gave her one of his sexy and very disarming smiles. 'Welcome to Didja, Lis.'

CHAPTER THREE

'I'LL let you know the blood test results as soon as I have them, Mrs Dittrich.' Melissa opened the door for her patient.

'I'm just a bit worried. This is my third baby, and the pregnancy is completely different from the others.'

'You've done the right thing by coming to see me.'

Mrs Dittrich stopped at the door and placed her hand on Melissa's shoulder. 'You have no idea how great it is to have a female doctor here. It's as though a collective feminine sigh has spread through the entire district. Finally we have someone who really understands us.'

'That's nice. Thank you.'

'Uhh…not that I'm suggesting that Dr Lawson or Dr Crawford are bad doctors. I'm not. It's just that—'

'It's fine,' Melissa interrupted with a warm smile. 'I understand completely. You take care, now.'

As Mrs Dittrich walked out of the consulting room Melissa saw Joss, standing on the other side of the corridor. She smiled, and he motioned a signal for drinking. She nodded and he headed off towards the kitchen.

Quickly she returned to her desk, scribbled a few notes in Mrs Dittrich's file and wrote out the official request for the blood test. When that was done she straightened the papers on her desk so it was nice and neat before heading to have a quick cuppa with Joss. Curiosity was coursing through her at the prospect of just being in the same room as him, and she dampened it down.

She needed to be careful, because she knew if she threw herself into life here in Didja, if she became too close to Joss too quickly, then she was bound to get hurt again. It was what had happened with her fiancé. They'd met, started dating, announced their engagement and called the wedding off all within six months. Moving fast hadn't worked. Trying to fill the void in her life with people simply for the sake of it hadn't worked either.

That was when she'd realised that, no matter what, she'd needed to find Dex. She'd needed to seek him out and have *him* in her life—because he wasn't just anyone…he was her brother. So she'd written to him, asking him to reconsider meeting her. It had taken a while, but she'd received a reply telling her if she wanted to come all this way to meet him, he wasn't going to stop her. Of course it wasn't exactly the reception she'd been hoping for, but the fact that he hadn't snubbed her completely was a good sign.

It appeared that the entire town was watching them—or at least watching *her*, at any rate. They were interested in how she and Dex were getting on. They were interested in the kiss she'd shared with Joss. And a few men had almost begged her to reconsider the kissing booth idea.

'So, how are things going with you and Dex? Any progress?' Bub had asked on New Year's Day, when Melissa had gone to the hospital to check on the three inpatients.

'Not really.'

'Did you know you were adopted?'

'I did. My parents never hid it from me.'

'That would have made things easy for you.

Well…easier, at any rate. Did they know you wanted to find your birth mother?'

'I didn't start searching for her until after both my adoptive parents had passed away. Although they wouldn't have stopped me if I'd tried any earlier.'

'Dex, as you may have guessed, hasn't taken the news of a new sister all that well. Josiah's been the one holding him together.'

'They're close?'

'Like brothers.' Bub grinned as she spoke. 'Closer than brothers. They've been through a lot together, and it was Josiah who convinced Dex to meet you.'

'It was?'

'Yep. Said that despite the past it wasn't *your* fault he'd been adopted, and that getting to know you would be a good thing.'

Melissa blew her fringe off her forehead. 'Well, Dex's done a great job of that so far. He's said hello and allowed me to treat him for a bump to the head. Real heart-warming stuff.'

'He needs lots of time.'

'And I've got twelve months of it to give.'

'Go to the pub at night. Dex's usually there after work. Chatting and the like. If you don't feel completely comfortable just walking into the pub like that, ask Josiah to go with you.'

'Joss usually goes to the pub at night, too?'

Bub shrugged. 'Five nights out of seven—give or take a day or two.'

'Does he have family in town or in the area?'

'Josiah? No, darl. His people are all in Perth or scattered around in the major cities.'

'I wonder why he came here in the first place?' Melissa pondered, and hadn't even realised she'd spoken the words out loud until Bub answered her.

'Why don't you ask him?'

'Huh?' Melissa's eyes widened with mortification. 'Oh. Well. It's really none of my business.'

'We're a small community, darl. All living in each other's pockets. Secrets don't usually stay secret for long. I will tell you, though, that when he moved to town he was a right little recluse. Didn't do him any good. One night, as we couldn't get him to the pub, we brought the pub to him.'

'What? Really? How did you do that?' She smiled, intrigued by the story.

'Everyone grabbed a beer and walked over to where Josiah was living at the time, which wasn't far away from the old clinic near the train station.

We all went down there with our beers, and Wazza hooked up a keg, and then we sat on the ground and made him come out to chat with us.'

'And did he?'

'Too darn right he did. Ya see, he was only getting to know us as patients, not as people, and in a community like this it's important to get to know the people first. This isn't some big hospital where everyone is a number. We respond better when we know that our docs are *really* interested in us—when we can get to know them, too. To see that they're just people and we don't need to be afraid of them.'

Melissa was surprised and a little confused. 'Is someone afraid of me?'

Bub shook her head. 'Ya missing the point, darl. The pub is like our community hall. Even though we actually do have a community hall,' Bub added as an aside, 'and we do use it—but that's not what I meant. At the pub we all gather and mix, and it's where we can all be ourselves. All equals. All needing to quench our thirst. Everyone's the same. From the lowest-paid to the highest. In the pub there's no hierarchy. There are just mates.'

Mates. Melissa had sighed over the word. It would be nice to have some more…mates.

Melissa had written up the new medication for her patients and then left Bub to care for them. She was an exceptional nurse, and also appeared to have her finger on the pulse of what was happening in the community. Taking her advice would be the right thing to do—and besides, it meant she could get to know her colleagues much better.

Her thoughts turned from Bub to Joss and the kiss they'd shared. A simple, ordinary New Year's kiss which had completely rocked her world. That had never happened to her before, and she had found it extremely difficult to stop thinking about it. The man made her tingle whenever she saw him—and now he was waiting for her in the kitchenette.

Tingles or not, he was her colleague, and hopefully her friend, and that was all there was ever going to be between them. She'd had one broken heart and she wasn't in the market for another.

Melissa took a deep breath and slowly let it out, effectively calming herself down before she rounded the corner into the kitchenette. The instant she saw him the tingles returned anew.

'Milk? Sugar?' he asked as he finished pouring her a cup of tea.

'Just milk, thanks.' She watched as he stirred the liquid in her cup before handing it to her. 'Ahh, thank you. I need this.' She walked over to the table and sat down, sipping gratefully at the tea.

'Busy?' Joss watched as she sat. She was dressed in a pair of three-quarter-length trousers which outlined her hips and slim legs. The top she wore was pale blue and highlighted her beautiful blonde hair, which was pulled back into a sensible ponytail. The scent she wore wound around him. It wasn't too strong, yet its subtle bouquet reminded him of the flower garden his mother had used to grow when he was a boy. Nostalgia combined with sex appeal. Oh, this woman was having too much of an effect on him.

He'd seen her in the corridor outside her clinic room and she'd looked tired. When she'd seen him standing there he hadn't wanted her to think he'd been watching her—even though he had. Internally panicking, he'd mimed drinking, and the grateful look which had crossed her face had made him feel a heel. So he'd made her a cup of tea—the one she was sipping right now, her pink lips blowing delicately on the hot liquid—and now that they were in the confines of the kitchenette together he was trying to figure out how to keep his distance from her.

'Yes. Very busy,' she answered.

Joss nodded and leaned against the bench, forcing his mind to stop concentrating on watching her. 'Happens.'

Melissa smiled, feeling a little odd with his monosyllabic conversation. 'It's just as well I'm used to a big workload.'

'Good.' For a moment Joss wondered what her life had been like back in Hobart. Had she dated anyone? Was she still involved with someone? He knew next to nothing about this woman who had been on his mind constantly since she'd arrived in Didja.

A silence fell between them. Joss sipped at his drink. Melissa did the same, trying desperately not to look at him. She glanced at the table, but there weren't even any magazines there that she could flick through.

'Is it usually this busy? Not that I'm complaining, you understand,' she added quickly.

He shrugged. 'Generally.'

Again silence. Melissa tried not to sigh with exasperation. He was the one who'd invited her in here to join him for a cuppa. What was the point if he wasn't going to talk to her? She could have made herself a drink and had it in the confines of her consulting room.

'Well, back in Hobart I worked at a few different places. I spent two days a week at the Women's and Children's Hospital, two days in Hobart at a private practice and two days a week at a King Island private practice.' She paused, realising she was only reiterating what he would have read on her résumé. 'King Island is one of the small islands between Tasmania and the mainland of Australia. Where they make the cheese.'

Melissa couldn't believe how badly she was babbling. Of course he knew where the cheese came from—and even if he didn't, why on earth would he care? Then again, he didn't seem to care about making any attempt at polite conversation. If this was the way it was going to be, it would turn out to be an exceedingly long year.

Joss nodded, which at least indicated he was listening to her rambling. Melissa looked away from him and took another sip of her drink, not caring that the liquid was scalding her throat. The sooner she finished this cuppa, the sooner she could get out of there and back to her job.

She decided to just sit there and ignore him. She'd done her bit. She'd tried to make conversation. If he wanted to stay here in silence, then that was just fine with her.

Joss watched as she sipped her tea, those lips of hers almost hypnotising him the way they were placed on the edge of the cup. His own drink was getting cold, but he didn't care. He placed it on the bench beside him and shifted his weight, wanting to talk to her, to find out more about her. It was dangerous territory, though, and he'd been stopping himself time and time again from going there. She was a colleague. That was all.

He cleared his throat. 'Do you have…? I mean—' He stopped and raked a hand through his hair. This was definitely unchartered territory, but he didn't seem to be able to stop himself from voicing the questions which had been running around in his mind for the past few days. 'Back in Tasmania, do you have…someone?'

She raised her eyebrows at that. Was this why he'd asked her in here? To probe into her private life? To find out more about her? If that was the case, he'd been doing a superbly bad job at it. And now this! 'Someone?'

'Are you seeing someone?' he finally managed to get out.

'Oh.' She grasped his meaning. 'Uh…no. I was—well, I was engaged.'

'Really?' Was she on the rebound? Suffering a broken heart? Had she decided she might as well search for her long-lost brother and get over her heartache at the same time? 'How long ago did it end?'

'Early last year.'

He frowned for a second. 'Wait. Early last year as in the year that ended three days ago, or the year before that?'

'Last year as in three days ago.' She sighed in exasperation. 'Why? Concerned that if I had someone waiting in Tasmania I might not stay for the whole twelve months? I'm contracted here, Joss. I honour my contracts, and it would take something really bad to happen for me to break this one.' She raised an eyebrow at him. 'Satisfied?'

She was angry with him. That much was

evident—even though it hadn't been his intention to annoy her. The woman was incredible to look at, she was smart, she was sassy, and he couldn't help but like her. That was the reason why it was imperative that he keep as much distance between them as possible and keep their relationship purely professional. 'What about family? Where are they situated?'

'Here.'

'Here?'

'In Didja.' Melissa's voice was clear, and this time Joss detected vulnerability in her words.

'But only Dex's in—' He stopped, his mind whirring too fast. His eyes opened a bit wider. 'Wait. Do you mean to tell me the only family you have is Dex?'

'Yes.'

'Only Dex?' He wanted to be clear on this.

'Yes.' Melissa put her half-drunk tea onto the table and took a breath, deciding to get the explanation over and done with as quickly as possible. 'My adoptive parents both died four years ago, and after two years of feeling all alone and miserable I decided to do something about it. So I contacted the adoption agency and tracked down my birth mother—Eva. It was then I learned about Dex. Until that time I had no clue I even had a brother, which is a shame as I was raised an only child. Anyway, Eva died about six months ago, and when Dex finally agreed to see me I wasn't about to look a gift horse in the mouth. There. Now you have it. My sorry little story.'

'Lis.'

His voice was rich and deep, just the way she liked. She could listen to him talk all day long in those sultry smooth tones. If she'd wanted to make him feel like a heel then she'd certainly succeeded. He pushed away from the bench and took a few steps towards her. 'Thank you for telling me.'

Her words had been matter-of-fact, as though she'd gone over the story in her head time and time again, but he was sure that deep down inside there was a lot of emotion stirring and bubbling away. He felt for her so much because he couldn't imagine what it would be like to be all alone in the world. With the large family he'd been raised in it was also an impossibility, but still, his heart felt for the brave woman before him. She'd been all alone—but she'd done something about it. His admiration for her increased.

'It's fine.' She watched as he walked slowly to stand beside her. Without a word, he reached out a hand and gently touched her face.

'You're really all alone?' His words were a mere whisper.

'Yeah.' Her answer was barely audible.

'There ya both are,' Areva, the receptionist, chided. Joss instantly dropped his hand back to his side and turned, walking away from her. 'What are you doing? Drinking the bores dry? Get back to work. There's hardly any room for the patients to sit down, there are so many of them in the waiting room.'

'Sorry,' they mumbled contritely before Areva left.

Melissa wanted to stand, wanted to take her cup to the sink, to rinse it out and then do as the receptionist had suggested and get back to work. Yet at the moment she wasn't at all sure even standing would be achievable, let alone doing anything else. The way Joss had looked at her, had touched her… Her heart was still pounding double-time. Masses of tingles had flooded through her body, creating more explosions than the fireworks had done the other night.

One look. One simple caress and her bones were a mass of jelly. At least the other night when he'd kissed her, when he'd tantalisingly brushed his mouth over hers, when his lips had met hers—hesitantly and politely at first, before realisation had dawned on both of them—at least then she'd had his arm around her for support. If she attempted to stand now she was certain she wouldn't be able to accomplish it and would end up in a heap on the floor.

Why did he have to be so confusing? One second he was monosyllabic, not seeming interested in being anywhere near her, and then he was asking her personal questions and caressing her cheek. She hadn't expected him to react the way he had when she'd told him her sad little story, and now she was more perplexed than before.

What on earth had he been thinking? Why had he touched her? He'd been doing really well, staying on the other side of the room, not engaging her in conversation. And then, for some ridiculous unknown reason, he'd gone and asked about her private life! What an idiot he was. What he should have done was excuse himself and take his drink back to his consulting room and get on with the work he loved so much. But, no. Instead he'd not only pried into her life but he had been so moved by what she'd said he'd been over-whelmed with compassion. He'd touched her. Touched that smooth, silky skin. And now he had that memory as well as the others to contend with. He shook his head, needing to get out of this room as soon as possible. Areva was right. They had work to do.

Dex strode into the kitchen, carrying his own cup to the sink, and it was as though he'd sliced through the intense atmosphere Melissa and Joss were trying to cope with. Interruptions were good. It was bad for herself and Joss to be alone like this. Part of her longed for it…to let go, to be free, to just throw caution to the wind and see where this attraction she felt for him might lead… But only part of her. The other part warned her against moving too fast, against be-lieving she could have a fairytale ending to her lonely little life. She'd been there and she'd done that, and for that reason alone she had to remain indifferent to Joss. But how?

'You two got in trouble,' Dex said, with a grin on his face. 'Areva told you off.'

'You are such a larrikin, Dex. You sound like an eight-year-old,' Joss commented, but he was secretly relieved to have his friend there to break the tension. He'd touched Melissa! He'd been so enthralled by her, so focused on wanting to feel that soft smooth skin of hers, on looking into those wide brown eyes to offer her compassion and comfort. Yes—Dex being here, teasing them, was just the ticket.

'Maybe I am eight years old. Maybe I was not only adopted, but born on the twenty-ninth of February, and no one's told me that, either.'

Joss felt the way Melissa winced at her brother's words and he bristled. 'That's enough. None of this adoption thing is Melissa's fault, so don't go taking it out on her.'

'Joss.' Melissa stood, pleased her legs were now able to support her. 'It's OK.'

'No.' Dex shook his head, his expression contrite. 'Joss is right.' He looked at her, and she saw in his expression that he was truly sorry for his words. 'That was rude. I'm sorry, Melissa.'

'It's OK,' she repeated, but this time smiled at

her brother. 'It's all a bit much to get your head around at times.'

As she spoke, she picked up her cup to carry it to the sink. Joss took four huge steps away from it, almost ending up in the doorway, to give her more than enough space to rinse her cup. Distance. He needed a lot of distance from her.

'Well, I'm up to date with *my* patients,' Dex commented, his tone and words striving to find some normality in all of this. 'It's you two having your little *tête-à-tête* that's putting you so far behind.'

'You just want to finish early so you can get to the pub on time,' Melissa teased. 'Don't tell me you want Bluey to give you another black eye?'

Both men chuckled at her words, and the air cleared to a happier atmosphere. Dex raised a hand to tenderly touch his eye and winced.

Melissa winced too. 'Does it still hurt? It should have started to heal by now.' Her voice was full of concern, but Dex's expression changed instantly to one of cheeky humour.

'I'm fine, but I really appreciate the concern.'

'You're most welcome. Any time you need genuine concern, come and see me.'

'Will do.' He paused and looked expectantly

at Joss. 'And if I need genuine favours I'll go and see Joss.'

Joss looked at his friend. 'No.'

Dex spread his arms wide. 'You don't even know what I'm going to ask!'

'I really do, and the answer is no.'

'But…'

'No.'

'Come on, mate. You know how I hate it.'

'Hate what?' Melissa felt as if she was at a ping-pong match, looking from one to the other.

'No.' Joss beckoned for Melissa to leave. 'We have patients to see, so we'd best get back to work,' Joss continued as he urged Melissa from the room. 'Don't want to keep them waiting any longer.'

'What was all that about?' Melissa asked as they walked towards their consulting rooms. He leaned a little closer, lest Dex should hear him, his breath fanning her neck and causing goose-bumps to race down her spine. Did the man have any idea the effect he was having on her?

'Dex hates house-calls.'

'He does?' Her eyes widened at this news, and in the next moment she flicked her gaze down to look at Joss's mouth. Big mistake. She shouldn't be looking at his mouth when they were this close to each other. Dangerous. Very dangerous.

'Yes, and he'll do anything to get out of going—so don't let him talk you around. Stand firm. Be strong.'

'You don't think I can resist him, do you?' The question was rhetorical, because she wasn't quite sure she would have been able to resist Dex if he'd asked her to swap with him, even though she wouldn't have had a clue what house-calls entailed out here in the Outback.

'At this stage? No. You're still in the excited stage at being so close to your brother.'

Melissa tried not to laugh at that, because she was in a bigger state of excitement simply because she was so close to *Joss*. The man obviously had no clue how his nearness was affecting her.

'You need to trust me on this. I know him a lot better than you, and you do not want to swap house-call shifts with him—because it doesn't end up being a swap; it ends up being you doing all of them.'

'Why doesn't Dex like house-calls? I thought he liked mixing with people.'

'He does. He's more than happy to see patients

here, and he'll chat with people in the pub, but going to their houses?' Joss shook his head. 'He'll do it, but only under duress.'

'So you put him under duress?'

'I have to. It's part of his job description. We take turns. It keeps it fair and stops us from burning out.'

'Fair enough.' Melissa decided it was best not to argue with the boss, although she was curious as to why her brother didn't like that one aspect of the job.

'In fact,' Joss continued as an idea dawned on him, 'it might be a good opportunity for you to go with him tomorrow. That way you'll get to learn the ropes of what's expected of us as far as Outback house-calls go. You'll also get to spend some time alone with Dex.'

Melissa considered the idea for a moment, liking what Joss was suggesting. It would also give her some time away from *him*, and hope-fully she'd be able to get herself better under control. Some distance was definitely what she needed, and she nodded enthusiastically. 'Sounds great. Oh, but what about my clinic?'

He waved her words away. 'We can reschedule

that. Patients have been waiting for quite some time to see you; waiting a few extra days won't hurt. Besides, I can see anyone who's urgent.'

Areva would not like him for suggesting such a plan, but if it meant he had the opportunity to put a bit of distance between himself and his new colleague then it would definitely be worth it. Melissa Clarkson was already taking up too much room in his private thoughts.

Thoughts of her had plagued him ever since he'd first laid eyes on her. Thoughts of her came into his mind, invading his otherwise organised mental patterns, at the most unusual times. Such as at three o'clock this morning. He'd been awoken by soft music and the sound of pacing. He'd listened, wondering if there was anything wrong. Was she sick? Did she require help? He'd sat up in bed, listening carefully to try and figure out what she was doing. He'd heard water go on and off in the bathroom. More pacing, more soft music, and then…soft sweet singing.

She was all right, and she had the singing voice of an angel.

He'd lain back in bed, hands behind his head,

eyes closed, and just listened. Her voice had been smooth and lovely, and soon he'd found himself drifting off into a deep and relaxing slumber. He hadn't slept like that in years.

Oh, yes. He'd been thinking about Melissa Clarkson far too much, and he wasn't at all sure what to do about it. He had no idea what she'd just said, and couldn't help it when his gaze flicked from her gorgeous brown eyes to her lips—only for a second, yet it felt like for ever. Those luscious lips of hers were plump and looked delicious. The urge, the desire to lean forward and press his mouth to hers, was only intensifying with every extra moment he spent alone with her, breathing in her sweet scent.

Melissa's mind had gone completely blank with that last stare from Joss. The air between them seemed to crackle with repressed tension—and she'd do well to keep it repressed. Her heart-rate increased, her lips parted, and she couldn't have stopped looking at him if the world had come crumbling down around them.

A noise from the waiting room made them both jerk backwards.

'House-calls with Dex tomorrow sounds

great,' Melissa reiterated, shifting towards her consulting room door.

'Right. I'll let him know and make arrangements for the rescheduling of your clinic.'

'Great.'

'Good.'

She couldn't believe how uncomfortable she felt, how aware she was of him, how she'd wanted him to kiss her again, right there in the middle of the corridor with a waiting room full of patients just around the corner.

Melissa pointed to her consulting room door. 'Best get back to it.'

'Yes.' Feeling ridiculous, and becoming cross with himself for yet again being unable to resist her allure, Joss turned on his heel and headed into his own consulting room, closing the door with a firm finality. 'And that is that,' he murmured.

Stalking to his desk, he sat down to go over the extra things he needed to tackle to get Melissa safely away with Dex tomorrow on the house-calls. First on the list was talking Dex into it, and he was sure his friend wasn't going to like the idea at all.

There was a knock at his door and in a moment

Dex strolled in, sitting in the chair opposite his friend and putting his feet up on the desk.

'Something I can help you with now that you've made yourself comfortable?' Joss asked, glaring pointedly at Dex's shoes.

Dex didn't remove them. 'I think you should do my house-calls this week.'

'The direct approach? Interesting.' Joss sat up straighter in his chair. 'No, Dex.'

'Aww, come on. What are friends for?'

'No, Dex.'

'It was initially your turn to do them anyway.'

'That's right, but I did yours three weeks running, which means it's now your turn, Dex.'

'But I promise to do your house-calls next week.'

'No, you won't.'

'You're right. I won't. Oh, well, how about I fill in for your clinic next week on my day off? That way you'll have time to show Melissa a bit more of Didja.'

'Still no.'

'In fact,' he pressed on, as though he hadn't heard his friend, 'you doing my house-calls this week would be a great way for you to show Melissa what it's all about.'

Joss nearly choked at the suggestion. Spending all that time alone, in such close quarters with Melissa? He hadn't been able to control himself in a small kitchenette. He hadn't been able to resist touching her. How was he supposed to cope in the smaller confines of the ute as they drove around the countryside? To Dex, however, he tried to remain completely unnerved. 'Actually, I was wanting to talk to you about that.'

'About you doing the house-calls with Melissa? Great idea. I accept.'

'That's not what I meant. I was talking about *you* doing the house-calls tomorrow with your sister. Get to know her better.'

'I can't take her. No. No siree.' He shook his head.

'She's your sister, Dex. You're going to need to open up to her sooner or later.'

'I choose later.'

'Dex, I under—'

'No. You don't understand, Joss. You have parents who are definitely your parents. You weren't lied to for almost thirty years by the people you love. You didn't find out—completely out of the blue—that you have an older sister, that you were adopted!' Dex thumped the desk.

Joss watched his friend. He hadn't seen him this riled-up for a long time.

Dex took a breath and calmed himself down. 'Look, I think it's great that she's here helping out at the clinic. Scoring ourselves an OB/GYN for a year was a great stroke of genius on your part and one of the major reasons I agreed to her coming. You are also right that it would be good for me to get to know her—just in case one day I need to ask for some bone marrow or a kidney or something. But right now it's just too soon for me to even be contemplating spending a whole day with her.'

Joss felt the walls start to close in on him, and wondered if he could try another tack at convincing Dex that spending time with Melissa was a good thing. There was no way *he* could do it. Such close quarters… That wouldn't be a way for him to get his libido back under control again.

'I know you've been hurt, Dex, but as I've pointed out before, none of this is Melissa's fault. Imagine how she's feeling. She comes to town to meet you, to get to know you, and you've hardly said two words to her.'

'I've said a few more than that,' Dex felt compelled to point out.

'It's like ripping a sticking plaster off. The sooner you get it over and done with, the better.'

'Why can't you take her? You're the boss here.'

'You're an equal financial partner, Dex.'

'But you run the show. You know I'm not good at the admin thing.'

'I know, and as the "admin thing" guy, I'm telling you it's your turn to do house-calls tomorrow, and Melissa will be accompanying you. End of story.'

'Ahh, but that's where you're wrong. You see, I think secretly, deep down inside, you really *want* to do these house-calls with Melissa tagging along. I think you *want* to get to know her better. I think you *want* to see if you can find some flaws, some faults—anything to help you to stop thinking about her.'

'What? What on earth are you talking about?'

'You like her.' Dex waggled his eyebrows up and down in an insinuating manner.

Joss ignored him and tried to keep his tone strictly professional. 'Of course I like her. She's a colleague.'

'That's not what I meant and you know it. You *like* like her. I saw you both before, in the corridor, making googly eyes at each other.'

Joss closed his eyes for a moment, unable to believe Dex had witnessed those few intense moments. But it was true, and there was no use denying it to his friend because Dex knew him far too well.

'This is good, Joss. You haven't been interested in any woman since Christina.' Dex leaned forward on the desk. 'If you like her, mate, you should do something about it.'

'She's your sister. She's a colleague. She's here to work. She has a year-long contract and I don't want anything to go wrong.'

'What if everything goes right? What if she's your Ms Right? You could marry her and we could end up being real brothers! That would be cool.'

Joss shook his head, knowing his friend was only joking. 'Funny. Very amusing,' he remarked without humour.

'But seriously, this is a good time for you to let go of the past and move forward into the future.'

'Hmm.'

'You need to let Christina go, Joss. Everything

that happened to you all those years ago is gone. Finished. Done. I never believed the allegations brought against you, and neither did your family. You were cleared of any charges and you moved on with your life—geographically, but not emotionally.'

'You're one to talk,' Joss commented. 'You haven't spoken to your family in how long?'

'This discussion isn't about me. It's about you. When, since you left Perth, have you ever been this interested in a woman? I'll tell you—never.'

'It's why I came to Didja in the first place. To get away from women. Besides, what if Melissa turns out to be like Christina? Ever think of that? What if she's all nice and lovely on the surface, but dig a little deeper and I might find something I don't want to know about?'

'Excuses, excuses. Believe me, I've used them all in my time. But this isn't about me; it's about you. You like her. You're attracted to her. That alone is enough of a reason to get to know her a little better. The past doesn't matter any more, and Christina wasn't any good for you anyway.'

'Apparently not.'

'You needed friends—true friends—to help build you up again, to support you.'

'And you were there.'

'That's right. And now you can be there for me by agreeing to do the house-calls this week.'

'Nice segué.' Joss shook his head and grinned at his friend. 'But my answer is still no.'

It had to be. He had to get his life back onto the nice even keel it had been in three days ago—before he'd ever laid eyes on Melissa Clarkson.

Dex's mobile phone rang and he broke off their debate in order to answer it. Joss mentally cooled his heels whilst he waited, going over the arguments in his mind. It was imperative he succeed. When Dex ended the call, he grinned very slowly at his friend.

'You look like the cat who ate the cream.'

'Oh, I have. I don't usually play dirty, but a man's gotta do what a man's gotta do.'

Joss's skin started to prickle with apprehension at his friend's words. 'Who was that on the phone?'

'The Watkinsons.'

Joss closed his eyes and buried his head in his hands, his shoulders instantly slumped in defeat. 'Oh, no.'

'Well you may cry, "Oh, no", my friend, because they're coming to Didja tomorrow. They'll be here for a whole week—and you know what that means.'

He wished Dex would keep quiet—that he'd go away. 'Can't you just gloat in private?' he asked, his words still muffled behind his hands.

'Nope. Besides, gloating is done much better in front of the person you wish to gloat about. I don't make the rules, mate, I just follow them. What a darn shame that the Watkinsons chose this particular weekend to come to Didja. What a darn shame that I need to be here to monitor their two children who have cystic fibrosis. What a darn shame I won't be able to do the house-calls tomorrow because I'll be needed here, at the hospital in town.'

'All right.' Joss sat up straight and squared his shoulders. 'All right. I'll do your house-calls tomorrow. But you are definitely going out next week and that's final. Nothing you can do will make me change my mind. Watkinsons or no Watkinsons.'

'Yes!' Dex punched the air.

'Get out.' Joss pointed to the door. 'Go on. Go gloat elsewhere. I have a lot of work to get done.'

Joss watched his friend almost dance his way out of the consulting room. When he was gone Joss shook his head, unable to believe the unlucky turn of events. Where he'd thought he'd have time away from Melissa, to control his wayward mind and body, it was now a matter of finding strategies which would see him through tomorrow.

He rubbed his jaw and exhaled slowly. Melissa was beautiful, funny and smart. Everything he'd ever wanted. Then again, Christina had been beautiful, funny and smart, and she'd ripped his heart out and crushed it. Although he was definitely attracted to Melissa, he'd also do well to be on his guard.

Women could lie. Women could be devious. Women were the reason he'd hibernated in the Outback for the past four years, keeping his distance from any sort of personal relationship. Yes, the sooner he discovered Melissa Clarkson's faults and flaws, the sooner he could move past this undeniable pull he felt towards her.

All that said, he desperately *wasn't* looking forward to tomorrow.

CHAPTER FOUR

BUB had told Melissa to pack an overnight bag whenever she went out on house-calls.

'It's just something we do out here in the Outback. You never know when the weather will turn. You could have buckets of rain coming down on you one moment and then bush fires the next. Sometimes you've gotta find shelter wherever you can, and other times you just go to the nearest farmhouse.'

'And people just let you stay?'

'Of course.' Bub had looked at her as though she was mad. 'We all support each other out here. You'll see lots of great scenery, maybe even some Aussie animals—we have quite a few emus out here. You'll meet new people, see how they all live, and be back in time to enjoy a coldie at the pub.' Bub had frowned as she'd spoken.

'Something wrong?'

'No. Not really. Just that I haven't seen Josiah down at the pub the past few nights. He's usually there. Hope he's not gonna start all that brooding stuff again.'

'He broods?'

'Oh, not for ages. But now and then, when his world is rocked from side to side, he tends to retreat back into his cave.'

'Cave?'

'A metaphor, darl. Never mind me. Off you go. Go pack your bag and get ready for tomorrow— and above all, enjoy yourself.'

Therefore Melissa had packed her overnight bag. In fact she'd packed and repacked it several times during the course of the evening. She'd been unable to sleep last night, so excited to be going out on house-calls with her brother. She would get to spend time with Dex, and even if he hardly spoke to her, just being with him, sitting beside him in the car, would be enough for her. It was happening. What she'd wanted for so long was finally coming true. She couldn't believe that her luck seemed to be changing.

With a smile on her face and a spring in her step, she made her way out of her apartment, checking she had the keys which Joss had given her. She closed the door, put her hat on her head and carried her overnight bag to the waiting ute.

'Joss!' She was surprised to see him up this early. Clinic didn't start for another two hours, so she'd presumed he'd still be sleeping. Instead, he was walking around checking the ute's fitted tarpaulin cover was securely in place.

He held out a hand. 'Your bag?'

Melissa handed over her bag. Joss didn't appear to be in a good mood at all, and she guiltily hoped she hadn't kept him awake last night with all her to-ing and fro-ing around the apartment due to her restless excitement.

Melissa looked around her. 'Where's Dex?'

'Sleeping.' Joss stowed her bag beneath the tarp before checking everything was secure once more. Then, much to Melissa's horror, he opened the driver's door and climbed in behind the wheel. Her eyes widened as she opened the passenger door.

'What are you doing?'

He looked across at her as though she were thick. 'Getting ready to drive.'

'But…but…where's Dex? Why is he sleeping?

You can't… You're not doing…' She stopped, her brain working overtime to cope with this change. Joss was doing the house-calls? She took a breath and tried to get herself under control. 'I thought I was doing house-calls with Dex.'

'Something came up.'

'He's not coming!' Didn't Dex want to be with her? Spend time with her? Was this her brother's way of telling her to stay away? That she could work here but she had to keep her distance as far as trying to have a relationship with him was concerned? Pain, hurt and rejection rose up within her.

'That's right. So if you get in we can get this day over and done with. And the sooner, the better.' He mumbled the last bit to himself, but Melissa had excellent hearing.

Melissa tried to swallow back the tears. Apparently neither of her colleagues wanted to spend time with her. Anger welled up inside. 'You don't want to do house-calls with me?' She stood outside the ute, stubbornly refusing to get in. 'Well, that's just fine. I can go out with Dex next week, and you can spare yourself from having to endure my company all day long. And if Dex doesn't want to go out with me next week, then write me a list of what I need to do and I'll figure it out on my own. Honestly, I'd heard all about Outback hospitality and how everyone here would make me feel welcome—well, between you and Dex I'm feeling about as welcome as a squashed bug on a windshield.'

Melissa shut the door and started walking away. Joss closed his eyes for a second, then hit the steering wheel. He climbed from the ute and hurried after her. It wasn't her fault Dex had changed the plan, and he felt like a heel. He'd let his unwanted attraction for her get in the way of his professionalism and now he'd made her feel bad. Joss knew what he had to do. He had sisters and he knew how temperamental women could be.

'Lis.' He reached out a hand to stop her, but she shrugged away his touch.

'You know, I just don't get you. One minute you're nice, and the next you're all Mr Tortured Soul and clamming up tighter than a…than a clam.' She turned to face him and pointed to the ute. 'It's a shame Dex doesn't want to do the house-calls with me, but you know what? That's OK. I can live with that. But this is part of my job and, quite frankly, I'd appreciate just a bit more professionalism on your part.'

Joss nodded. 'You're absolutely right, and I apologise for my behaviour.' He shifted his feet and shoved his hands into the pockets of his khaki shorts. 'Dex has to stay here and monitor a family who are coming to town. Two of their kids have CF and he's the expert in that field.'

'Oh.' So it wasn't just the fact that he hadn't wanted to spend time alone with her. Melissa started to feel bad about her outburst. This would have meant that Joss would have had to do some pretty fancy footwork in rearranging schedules. Still, one of them could have let her know about the change.

She could feel her anger draining and tried to hold on to it. When she was angry with Joss she didn't have to worry about fighting the attraction she felt for him. She wasn't particularly looking forward to spending all day with him in the close confines of the ute. They could hardly cope within the close confines of the kitchenette. Still, she was a professional, and this was part of her job. Whether she liked it or not, she'd be spending the day with Joss.

He held out his hand, indicating the ute. 'Shall we?' His tone was calmer, more reasonable, and she could see the business mask he wore was back in place. 'We have a busy day to get through, so the sooner we get rolling, the sooner we'll be back and having a drink at the pub.'

Melissa nodded, and the two of them returned to the waiting vehicle and climbed in, buckling their seat-belts. 'So, boss. Where's our first port of call?'

'Interesting that you should use a sailing metaphor out here, where there is barely any water at all.' Joss was driving the ute onto the main road of the town. 'Our first "port of call", as you term it, is the mine headquarters site office. It's only fitting that you get to meet the head honchos in their official capacity, even though you've probably seen them around the town, and you also need to get a glimpse of what the mine is all about.'

'Looking forward to it.' As they drove, the buildings of the town became few and far between. It was as though there was an invisible line and houses couldn't be built beyond it, because suddenly Melissa looked around and there were only small green shrubs mixing with the red-orange dirt at the side of the road.

After a while Joss turned right and headed down another seemingly endless road, and soon, as the signage depicted, they were upon the mine's security gate. After signing in, Joss parked next to a few other cars. As a way of making up for his bad behaviour earlier, Joss came around the car to open Melissa's door, but she beat him to it.

'Problem?' she asked, seeing him round her side of the car.

'Uh…no.' He felt self-conscious. 'I was just going to open your door for you.'

'Really?' Her eyebrows hit her hairline in surprise. 'Do you mean to tell me that chivalry isn't dead? Even out here in the middle of nowhere?'

'That's exactly it.' His expression was deadpan, but she thought she detected a slight twinkling of laughter in his eyes.

'In that case, then, I'll let you make it up to me by allowing you to open the door to the building.'

'Oh, thank you, Dr Clarkson. You're too kind.'

'And, should it ever rain here, make sure you have your coat handy. I loathe standing in puddles.'

He dutifully held the door open, waiting for

her to precede him. 'Duly noted, Dr Clarkson,' he murmured as they headed towards the reception desk.

The area was still half-decked in tinsel and baubles as the woman behind the desk was in the process of taking them down.

'Hello, Joss,' she said over her shoulder as she came down off a stepladder. 'Happy New Year to you.' She was bright and bubbly, her yellow badge declaring her name was Veronica. She wore a floral dress, had short grey hair and had a pen pushed behind her ear. 'And to you as well…Melissa, isn't it?'

'It is.' They both returned her greeting.

'There hasn't been an emergency, has there? I haven't been notified of one.' She walked to her desk and shuffled a few pieces of paper around.

'No, Veronica. No emergency. I've brought Dr Clarkson here to introduce her around and to help give her a bit of a bird's eye view of the mine.'

'Good idea. Well, it's lovely to see you again, Melissa.'

'Again?'

'We met on New Year's Eve. You probably don't remember. It's difficult when you're the new girl in town.' The phone on the desk started ringing. 'Go on through. Both Jeff and Scott are in there somewhere.' Veronica answered the phone as Joss led Melissa through a door and down a corridor.

'Have I met Jeff and Scott? Can you remember? It's really quite disconcerting when people know you but you don't have a clue who *they* are.'

Joss shrugged. 'I'm not sure.' Although he was sure she would have remembered meeting Scott. If Dex was the charming rogue in their community, Scott was most definitely the womaniser. If Scott had tried to sleaze Melissa at New Year's, the woman would have remembered.

They went through into a different office, Joss not bothering to knock as he opened the door. Two men were sitting at a large conference table, papers strewn before them.

'Joss.' One of them looked up.

'G'day, fellas. Just wanted to officially introduce you to our new doctor.'

'Excellent.' The two men came over and shook her hand warmly. Scott, however, held on to Melissa's hand for a bit longer than was necessary.

'When Jeff told me how incredibly beautiful

you were I was immensely sorry I hadn't stayed in Didja for New Year. I've been in Perth,' he volunteered. 'Still, it's a real pleasure to have you join our little community, Melissa. A real pleasure.' He shook her hand slowly as he said the last few words, and then with a great reluctance let her go.

Joss was trying not to seethe at the lecherous way Scott was looking at Melissa. If he needed to appoint himself her official protector then so be it. All for the good of the clinic, of course.

'Well…thank you.' Melissa stepped back, wanting to put a bit of distance between herself and Scott and accidentally bumped into Joss. He steadied her with a hand at her waist, letting it linger for a desperate moment before he dropped it back to his side.

As Jeff talked, telling her about the mining operation and pointing to the photographs on the wall which showed her exactly what the open cut mine looked like, Melissa was only conscious of the fact that Joss was still quite close to her.

That brief touch of his hand on her back had left a heated imprint, and the spicy scent he wore was starting to drive her to distraction. Why was she so interested in him? How did this attraction, which seemed to have come from nowhere, consume her so much?

Even when they headed out of the office so she could see the actual mine itself, she was highly conscious of every move Joss made. They went outside and walked down a set of stairs to the viewing platform, all of them standing there doing the time-honoured Australian salute of swatting flies, looking over the mining operation. Jeff and Scott pointed out the different aspects of the job, but all Melissa was conscious of was the nearness of her colleague. The platform was quite small, and therefore he couldn't really keep his distance. The heat from his torso was more prominent than the hot sun shining down on them, and it was affecting her equilibrium in ways the sun never could.

Melissa hoped to goodness that she nodded and murmured in the correct places, but knew she would probably have to research the entire mining operation on line, when Joss wasn't around to distract her.

They didn't spend too much time watching the enormous trucks—one or two of them with tinsel still wrapped around their antennae from Christmas—carting the mined rock up and down incredibly steep slopes which led in and out of the earth. Instead they headed back inside, away from the heat and the flies.

'Would you both like to stay for a drink?' Scott asked when they were back in the conference room. 'It's a bit of a scorcher out there at the moment.'

Melissa looked to Joss, unsure what their next move was. He was the boss, and today she was dancing to his tune.

'Sorry,' Joss replied a moment later, wanting to get Melissa as far away from Scott as possible. Honestly, the man had been giving Melissa such a come-on the entire time they'd been out on that platform. Joss hadn't liked it one bit. 'We need to get going. Have to get out to the Etheringtons, with quite a few stops to make along the way.'

'That's a lot of ground to cover,' Jeff remarked.

'His missus about ready to pop yet?' Scott asked.

Joss's smile was tight. 'Not yet, but that's one reason why I needed Melissa here to come along. Given that she's a qualified obstetrician, she'll be able to make sure everything is progressing well as far as mother and baby are concerned.' Joss turned to Melissa. 'Ready?'

It was strange, but even when he looked at her like that, one simple word coming from his lips, all she was aware of were his blue eyes, and the way they seemed to convey a multitude of unspoken words—especially when he lifted his eyebrows in such a cute and inquisitive manner. Talk about mixed signals and total confusion!

'Ready,' she confirmed.

They said their goodbyes and as they drove away from the open cut mine the atmosphere in the car descended into an uncomfortable silence. He wasn't at all sure what to say or do. He wanted to know if she'd been attracted to Sleazy Scott or whether she really hadn't given him a second glance. Only the last time they'd talked on personal topics he'd ended up caressing her cheek—a soft, gentle touch which still tortured him late at night. He had to come up with some sort of conversation—after all they had a good long drive to their next house-call, and that was a lot of time to fill with just silence.

It had been an age since he'd last been out with

a woman, and even then it had been a double date which Dex had basically forced him to attend. It was then he'd realised it would be extremely difficult to date seriously when you were a doctor in a small community. If the relationship didn't go right, then everyone in the community had an opinion on it. Add to all of that the fact that he'd never met anyone in Didja who affected him the way Melissa did—never had he felt such an instant attraction as he did with his new female colleague.

He knew she'd come to town to get to know Dex, but Dex hadn't been as receptive as she'd hoped. Was she therefore using him as a stop-gap until she could get attention from her brother? There had to be a hidden agenda somewhere. Christina had taught him that much at least.

Joss glanced again at Melissa. There was no denying the attraction he felt for her—as unexpected as it was—but could he risk taking a chance on a relationship? How would she react when she learned about his past? Would she reject and betray him as Christina had? He shook his head, forcing the thoughts away, and reminded himself that perhaps he was misreading the signals from Melissa. When he'd touched his hand to the small of her back, purely in order to steady her, he'd felt such a strong warmth course up his arm and explode throughout his body. Why did he have to be so attracted to her?

He decided some conversation had to be better than the present path his thoughts were taking.

'So…'

Melissa broke the silence before he could get a chance. Darn it. Was this yet more evidence that they were on the same wavelength? Joss had just decided to start a conversation about the weather, because the weather was definitely a safe topic.

'Tell me,' Melissa continued. 'What are your future plans for the clinic?'

'The clinic?' That was a safe topic too. He could do that one.

'You know? The place we work at? The one you've built from scratch?'

'Oh. *That* clinic.' Yes, talking about work was a very safe topic indeed. 'Plans. Hmm… Well, we have three doctors here now. That's a start. I do the odd surgical case—just small things. Dex does the anaesthetics, and now that you're here you'll be taking over the delivery of babies.'

'All you need is a paediatrician and you'll have a full house. That should round the team off nicely.'

'Do you honestly think we could get a paediatrician to come all the way out here? On a permanent basis?' He spoke as though she'd asked him to capture the moon. 'It was difficult enough trying to coax a female doctor out. We'd advertised for well over a year before we received your application.'

'Oh, great,' she joked. 'You're telling me I only got the job because I was the only applicant?'

'That's not what I'm saying,' Joss remarked. 'If your credentials hadn't been up to scratch the clinic wouldn't have employed you.'

'I see.'

'Honestly, Lis.' He looked across at her. 'You were hired strictly on your merits, I assure you. The fact that you wanted to come to town anyway to get to know Dex was simply a bonus.'

'And you knew I wanted to spend longer than three to six months in Didja because of Dex?'

'I did. You can't blame a guy for using it to his own advantage.'

'And I don't.'

She watched him surreptitiously as he drove, admiring his strong profile. He was so different from Renulf, especially in looks. Renulf was fair, yet Joss was dark. Renulf hadn't been able to make her knees turn to mush with just one look, yet Joss could. Renulf had never made her swoon with the merest brush of his lips across hers, and Joss had.

She knew it wasn't right to compare them but she couldn't help it. The man sitting next to her was well-liked and respected in the community, and he was most certainly good with the patients. Joss was so vibrant, so powerful and so incredibly handsome. She couldn't help the way he made her feel, but she *could* control her own reaction. Couldn't she?

'We're all motivated in different ways, and sometimes circumstances are the biggest dictators in our lives.'

He glanced at her. 'A deep comment.'

'You'd expect it from a woman who's watched everyone she ever really loved die.' Melissa swallowed over the lump which had immediately appeared in her throat.

'It must have been really difficult for you.'

'It was. Still is in a lot of ways.' She shook her head quietly. 'It's not easy being alone.'

'Why didn't it work out with your fiancé?' The instant the question was out of his mouth he wondered if he'd pushed a little too far, too fast. But if he wanted to get to know her faults and flaws it meant he had to dig a little deeper beneath the surface, and surely that meant getting a little bit more personal.

'Many reasons. I think it all boiled down to the fact that we didn't really have a strong foundation. Everything sort of happened rather quickly.' She took a deep breath, glad she had herself more under control now. 'How about you? There must have been something big happen in your life to make you settle in Didja.'

'I thought you weren't all that interested? At least, that's what you told me on your first day in town.'

'I'm interested, all right. I just wasn't as curious then as I am now."

'So you haven't heard the gossip, then?'

'There's gossip about you? No. I guess I must have missed it—although Bub did mention that you were quite reserved when you first came to town. How when you wouldn't go to the pub to have a drink with them, they brought the pub to you.'

The smile which crossed his lips was a slow one, and he nodded as memories returned. 'They did at that. I'd forgotten. It was a defining moment for me. One when I knew I needed to start letting go of the past if I was going to have any sort of decent future.'

'You're a man, all alone, working from dawn to dusk, and people only throw themselves into their work when everything else has gone to the dogs.'

'Gone to the dogs?'

'Or down the toilet. Choose the expression you like best.'

'How about up in flames?' Joss was sort of joking, but she heard the hint of pain behind his words. His hands gripped the steering-wheel tighter, his knuckles going white.

'It was that bad?' Melissa's tone was one of instant concern and compassion, and she couldn't help but reach over and give his hand a little stroke.

Joss was startled by her touch, but he didn't ignore it either. He glanced over at her, a multitude of pain reflected in those gorgeous blue depths, and she felt for him. 'It was.'

'Joss. I'm sorry.'

'For what? You didn't do anything.' He focused his eyes back on the very long, very straight road, not a house in sight, and pushed his foot down on the accelerator. The sooner they got to the next house, the better—because being confined with her like this, with her scent driving him crazy, with her gentle and soothing words affecting him, with her touch breaking through his reserve, was simply dangerous.

'I'm sorry for the pain you felt. Pain is never easy to go through—both physically and psychologically. After my adoptive parents died I was forced to do a lot of growing up. I learned the hard way about regrets, about life in general. We only have one life. One life which can end so quickly. Is the angst and frustration of fighting with the past really going to help with the future, or is it simply easier just to let it go and move on?' Melissa spoke as though talking to herself, perhaps trying to convince herself to let go of her own past.

They were quiet for a while, both seemingly lost in their own thoughts. Once more Melissa broke the silence. 'I thought we'd see a lot more kangaroos out here.'

Joss relaxed a little at the general topic of conversation, his hands loosening on the wheel, holding it more comfortably now. 'You'll see plenty of roos while you're out here, and emus. They love to race along with the car.'

'Sounds scary and fun at the same time. Don't they ever run into the car?'

'It has happened, but only on the odd occasion. Generally, I think they just want a race. Show-offs.'

Melissa smiled at his remark. The atmosphere in the car had returned to a more normal level of tension. They were able to chat more freely and relax a bit more. She asked him about the town and the patients they were going to see, the car eating up the kilometres as they talked, and it was nice and friendly, with neither wanting to spoil the sort of truce they'd found.

When Joss's cellphone rang it startled them both, but he quickly connected the call by tapping the earpiece connection around his ear. 'Joss here.' He listened intently, then checked the clock on the dashboard.

'We're about five minutes away from you.' A pause. 'Right. If you think it's that bad, then call Dex at the clinic and get him to liaise with the Royal Flying Doctor Service. Put them on stand-by for now, until I can take a look at the situation.' He disconnected the call and put his foot down on the accelerator. There were no speed limits out here—just long straight roads which seemed to stretch on for miles.

'Problem?'

'Murphy's Farm. One of the bulls has broken free from its pen and is on the rampage.'

Melissa's eyes widened. 'Bull? Rampage?' What was she doing out here? What if she'd been alone doing these house-calls? She didn't have experience with rampaging-bull wounds! 'Is it safe? Should we be driving around here? This fast?'

Her feelings must have been apparent because Joss quickly reassured her. 'Relax. You won't need to do any bull-wrangling today. Maybe next time, but not today.'

'Any casualties?'

'Yes. Two of the station hands have been injured. Rich thinks their wounds will require surgery, but we can assess that when we get there.'

She nodded. 'Sometimes there's more blood than injury.'

'Exactly.' Joss started to slow the ute, before turning onto what looked like a dirt paddock with a few tyre tracks on it. 'You all right with this?'

'What? The new road you're intent on making, or the rampaging bull we might literally run into?'

He chuckled again. 'I meant the injuries we're going to assess. Your résumé said you'd worked in A&E, so you should be experienced in emergency situations, right?'

'I'm highly proficient—although I will say that I've never treated a patient with rampaging-bull wounds.' She put out one hand to the dashboard and one to the ceiling as they bounced around; the ground was highly uneven.

'Aren't you glad I brought the ute with the good suspension?' Joss was clearly enjoying himself.

'I am. Where are we going?'

'Short cut. This way you'll only need to jump out and open two gates instead of five.'

'Out? Gates? Do I need to remind you there is a rampaging bull out there?' She went to point, to indicate the area they were driving through, but needed to hold on instead.

'He's heading in the other direction, if that makes you feel any better.'

'How do you know where the bull is?'

'Because Rich has a chopper in the air, tracking the animal. That bull is worth an awful lot of money, Lis, and whether it's angry or not Rich isn't going to let it out of his sight. So, unless you see a chopper in the sky, we'll be as right as rain.' Joss glanced up at the sky. 'And, speaking of rain, it looks as though we might actually get a few drops here and there.'

Melissa also peered up at the sky, and saw that there was quite a lot of cloud coverage out here—and they weren't the nice white fluffy ones. 'Is that what they mean by scattered showers?'

Joss chuckled. 'I just hope Dex hasn't been doing his rain dance.'

'His what?' She was clearly intrigued and surprised.

'Rain dance. Once he went outside first thing in the morning and did an official rain dance along with Nev and Kev, in the hopes that the roads would be so impassable that he wouldn't have to do his house-calls.'

'Did it work?'

'Amazingly, it did. That afternoon, when he was supposed to leave, Didja had its first rains in about five months. It rained for three days straight. Roads were impassable everywhere.'

Melissa giggled in disbelief at the antics of her brother. 'That's astounding. You could hire him out to those remote areas of the country which are most affected by the drought.'

Joss grinned at her, and she almost melted at the sight. 'I'd never thought of it that way before.'

'Well, here's hoping he hasn't been doing his rain dance. The last thing we need today is a bucketing downpour.'

Because if that happened, it could mean that the roads would become impassable, and if that happened it could mean that she and Joss would have to alter their plans for the day, and if that happened they might find themselves alone and in a highly secluded situation. And if that happened there was no telling exactly *what* might happen!

CHAPTER FIVE

WHEN they finally pulled up in front of the homestead, Joss was out of the ute like a shot. He grabbed the medical kit from the back of the tray as Melissa came around to stand beside him. 'We'll examine the station hands, and if necessary we'll get the RFDS out here. Chances are those men will need a transfer to the clinic's hospital.'

'Bub will have two new patients to fuss over.'

Joss smiled at her words, pleased she was getting to know the staff at the clinic. 'Yes, she will.' He was heading up the front steps of the homestead as they talked.

'OK. So where do we find our patients?' Melissa asked.

'No doubt around the back. We can take a short cut through the house.' He opened the front door and just walked right in, leaving a more hesitant Melissa to follow. She glanced up at the sky, noting the still gathering clouds as well as a sort of far-off buzzing noise. It was as though there was a giant mosquito around, yet she couldn't see it.

'The chopper,' she realised aloud as she went through the front door of a stranger's house. She wasn't sure where Joss had gone, so made her way tentatively through the comfortably furnished rooms.

'Oh, there you are, Melissa. Come this way. Joss told me to keep an eye out for you.' She was bustled through the house by a petite pregnant woman with lovely blonde hair and smiling green eyes. 'I'm Amanda, but everyone calls me Mindy. Come through. They're out the back.' As they went through the house, Melissa heard the chopper getting closer. 'I hope they find that bull, because I want to give it a piece of my mind.'

'Really? You want to tell a bull off?'

'Oh, he's really not that bad—and we do need him. He's a good source of income—breeding-wise,' she finished as they walked through the kitchen towards the back door. 'I could tell he was going to fly off the handle. Rich thought I was mad—kept telling me that I couldn't read a bull's mind.'

'And can you?' Melissa was intrigued by this woman as they headed outside to the rear of the homestead. She shielded her eyes from the glare of the sun as she looked around, searching for Joss. Mindy kept on walking so she kept on following.

'I have this intuition thing where animals are concerned.' She turned and grinned brightly at Melissa. 'Rich says that's why I married him. He's such an animal. Anyway, it's just a thing. I can tell when the animals are jittery or a bit off.' She shrugged. 'I've always had it, and my dad came to rely on it. Rich still has a lot to learn. We've only been married for three years, but he'll get there.'

'Perhaps after today he'll listen more carefully and we won't have more casualties.'

'True.' Mindy was serious again. 'I hope the boys are all right.'

'Boys?' Had some children also been hurt?

'The two guys who just weren't fast enough when the bull decided to have a temper tantrum. You'd think they'd be a little bit quicker on the uptake.' They rounded a corner near the back shed and there were the 'boys'. Joss was kneeling down next to one of them; the other man was propped up against the side of the shed in the shade, a bandage around his upper arm and shoulder.

'Do you think we'll need the RFDS?' she asked as she knelt down on the other side of the patient.

'Yes. I'd like the patients in at least overnight for observation.' He gestured to the medical kit. 'I need Vicryl sutures, double zero and zero.' He'd pulled on gloves and was just finishing injecting a local anaesthetic near the wound site. 'James here has been very lucky indeed. That bull only gave him a bit of a love nick.' Joss indicated the gash in the station hand's abdomen. 'A little to the right and you might have lost a kidney, mate.'

'So long as he wasn't initiating a mating ritual, I'll be right,' James added with a laugh, then winced in pain.

'Take it easy,' Melissa soothed. 'What analgesics have they been given?'

'I've just given them both morphine,' Joss answered. 'James here is worse than Andy, and Mindy's had a good look at Andy and applied bandages.'

Melissa went and took a closer look at Andy, checking his pupils and reflexes, listening to his heartbeat, taking his blood pressure and counting the beats of his pulse. 'You're doing just fine, Andy,' she reassured him when she was finished, then stood and looked at Mindy. 'Good work,' she praised. 'Nice pristine bandaging.'

Mindy shrugged. 'I've had experience.' At Melissa's raised eyebrows, Mindy elaborated. 'This is my farm. It's where I grew up. Rich was the foreman for years—that's how we met—and when my dad passed away last year Rich just took over. Growing up on a farm like this, out in the middle of nowhere, means you have to be prepared for anything. So I've done first aid courses and cooking courses and bookkeeping courses and several other courses to make sure I can handle anything that's thrown at me.'

'Impressive.'

Mindy wrinkled her nose and rubbed her stomach. 'I just wish they offered parenting courses on line, too.'

Joss looked up from where he was getting ready to debride James's wound. 'Given the way you keep all these blokes in line, I don't think you're going to have any trouble being a parent, Mindy.'

'That's what Rich says.'

'Then you should listen to him. I'm almost ready, Lis.'

'OK. So how do I contact the RFDS? Do I just call Dex and get him to organise it all?'

'Yes. Murphy's Farm. Two patients requiring transfer. Give him the particulars of the injuries and he can organise Phemie and her crew.'

Melissa nodded and made the phone call, giving Dex the particulars, all the while quite excited about her first contact with the Royal Flying Doctor Service. She'd heard so much about the people who ran it—most of the Didja locals heralded them as true Outback heroes—and now she was delighted at the opportunity to meet them. Although she most certainly wished the circumstances were different.

'Right.' Joss turned his attention to Melissa. 'Ready when you are, Lis.'

Melissa came over and knelt down on the opposite side of James, pulling on a pair of gloves. 'Ready, boss.'

She wanted to ask why they couldn't move James to a more sterile location. She wanted to know how they were supposed to keep the multitude of buzzing flies away from the patient, the wound and themselves as they treated him. However, Joss was ready to do what he did best, and as he had obviously done it quite a few times before, she wasn't about to question him. She'd come to an Outback clinic, and all of this was about learning how to do things the Outback way. If it meant improvising then they would improvise, and she would learn how.

'OK. If you can start by putting an IV line in. Saline is in the medical kit. Mindy, we're going to need something to hang a drip bag on.'

'I can hold it,' Mindy offered.

'No.' Melissa and Joss spoke in unison.

'You need to be in the shade if you're outside, and preferably off your feet. Get me a chair or, better yet, stick a pitchfork in the ground. Anything we can use to hook the bag over but keep it elevated.'

'I'm on it,' she called as she waddled off to the shed. By the time she returned Melissa had the needles and tubes in and was ready to connect it all.

'How are you holding up, James?' she asked.

'All the better for looking up at you,' he murmured, with a silly grin on his face.

Melissa raised her gaze and looked at Joss, who smiled back. 'I'd say the analgesics are working just fine,' Joss said.

'Why? Because he'd have to be out of it to find me attractive?' She pretended to bristle.

'No.' Mortification laced his words, but then he relaxed as he realised she was teasing. 'I only meant that usually James isn't one to speak like that—especially to a woman he's only just met.'

'He's right,' Mindy clarified. She shooed some flies away as she sat down on the ground near James's head. 'Mind if I watch?'

'Not at all,' Joss replied, and, now satisfied that the local anaesthetic had taken effect and that James was not in any pain, he began the procedure of tidying things up and stitching them closed.

Melissa noted that even with the less than ideal circumstances Joss was being quite thorough. His careful thoroughness suggested that he was an excellent surgeon, and she wondered how many times he'd had to treat patients in such remote circumstances like this. As she took a quick second to glance around, it struck her just how far away from 'civilisation' they really were. It was one thing to come all the way to a small Outback practice to try and get to know her brother, but now that she was here there was a small niggling doubt that perhaps she'd bitten off more than she could chew. Would she be able to last twelve months as an Outback doctor? And what would happen after that?

'That will do him for now. I'll take a closer look later, once he's settled at the hospital.' Joss looked down at their patient. 'How are you doing, James?'

'Sleepy.'

'Any pain?'

'Nope.' They all smiled at the way he said the word.

'OK. I'll check Andy again, if you wouldn't mind doing obs on James.' Joss changed his gloves and crouched down near Andy.

'How are *you* doing?'

'Fine.'

'No pain?'

'I'm cool. Just a nice gentle buzz.'

'No. That's the flies, mate.' Joss grinned at his patient, then looked at Mindy. 'Mindy, I'm loath to undo your clean bandaging, so if you could tell me what the wound looked like, that would be great.'

'The gash to his arm was fine once I cleaned it with a bit of saline. I had some special bandage stuff which is supposed to be good for things that might only need one or two stitches.'

'Steri-strips?' Joss asked, and she nodded.

'That's what I put on his arm, and then the bandage. His head was a similar story, but the gash wasn't as deep. James took the major brunt as far as gouging goes, but Andy whacked his head pretty badly.'

'You saw the whole thing?' Melissa raised her eyebrows as she finished James's observations.

'I did. I was at the kitchen window and I can see out as far as the paddock. They were bringing the bull in and he was just in a bad mood. You know—we all have bad days. I told Rich this morning that I'd come and help, but he forbade me to go anywhere near the bull—because of the baby.'

'A wise decision—especially given the circumstances.'

'Chest is clear.' Joss held up his finger and got Andy to track it. 'Perfect.' Joss looked over at Mindy. 'What happened next?'

'I grabbed the medical kit—I always keep it fully stocked by the back door—and went out to help. The bull was still pounding around, with everyone running clear so they didn't get trampled. Then the bull turned and ran the other way, barging through the corral fence. It just took off.'

Thunder started to rumble in the distance.

'Do you think it might have been the approaching storm?' Melissa asked. 'Some animals do have a real sixth sense where the weather is concerned.'

'You could be right. It wouldn't surprise me,' Mindy responded. 'I hope they find him.' She looked out into the distance, wanting to see her husband returning, bull securely roped and chastised for his behaviour.

'Right. Andy, I want you in Didja as well. I want head X-rays, and then we'll take a better look at those gashes tomorrow.'

'Is it necessary?' Andy asked quietly. 'I mean, poor Rich is going to be without James as it is.'

'Let's just say you need to be in hospital. You can leave this time tomorrow, but only if everything checks out. Head injuries are funny things. Symptoms can be masked for quite a while. You tell either one of us—' he indicated Melissa and himself '—if you feel queasy, or as if you're going to be sick. Any pounding headaches, you let us know. Understand?'

'Yes, Joss.'

'Good. If you feel sick on the plane, you tell Phemie. And if you feel sick when you're at the hospital you tell Bub or Dex.'

'Yeah. I get it,' Andy remarked.

'You'd better. Head injuries are serious business. Don't you dare go all macho and put up with the pain.' He looked down at their patient for another moment before nodding, hoping the message had really got through to the jackaroo. He stood and pulled off his gloves, folding them together. He gathered up their garbage, accepting Melissa's gloves from her, and put everything into the bin. 'Now, Lis, why don't you and Mindy go inside and get her check-up done. I'll call Dex again to check on the arrangements and give him an update. We still have a few more places to visit before the day is over.' He glanced up at the sky. 'And the sooner we can get under way, the better.'

Melissa did as she was told, gathering her own medical bag of tricks and going inside, relieved to be out of the heat. Mindy led the way into the bedroom, where she sat on the bed and rolled up her sleeve so Melissa could take her blood pressure.

She took out the portable sphygmomanometer and wound the cuff around Mindy's arm. 'How has everything been progressing with your pregnancy?'

'Good. No swelling of the ankles, hands or feet.'

'Good.'

'I have my own blood pressure monitor here, and the readings have been within normal limits.'

'Excellent.' Melissa waited for her own reading and indeed found that Mindy's blood pressure was just fine. 'No other problems? Indigestion? Insomnia?'

'Mild to fair. Nothing out of the ordinary.' Mindy paused for a second and looked at Melissa. 'I'm just so glad you've come to town. I'd much rather go to Didja to have my baby than to Perth.'

'Is that where you would have gone?'

'Oh, yes. Most women when they reach about thirty or thirty-five weeks pack their bags and head off to Perth. They have to stay with friends or family, and apart from going to doctor's appointments they just sit around in a strange place and wait for their baby to arrive. If things are bad they have to stay in hospital—sometimes from the end of the first trimester.'

'A lot can go wrong with pregnancies,' Melissa murmured, but her mind was whirring. She hadn't really thought about it before. All those women having to leave their loved ones at a time when they needed their support more than ever. She was here now to provide obstetric assistance to the women of the community, but what would happen after her contract ended? Would Joss be able to get another obstetrician out here, or would the women have to go back to leaving their families at such a crucial time? It was definitely something to ponder.

'Some women,' Mindy continued, 'opt to have their babies at home, with just other women helping out with the delivery—mainly Rajene; she's like an unofficial midwife. But...' Mindy screwed up her nose at the idea. 'So much can go wrong, as you've said. However, Gemma Etherington seems to like it. She's had her last four at home and nothing went wrong—but she does have six children, so it's not as though she doesn't know what she's doing.'

Melissa listened, intrigued by the plight of these tough Outback women. 'We're headed to their place this afternoon.'

'Gemma's pregnant with number seven.' Mindy smiled. 'You'll find a lot of big families out here in the back of beyond. I guess people think we have nothing better to do with our time than to farm and have kids.'

'Do *you* want a healthy brood?'

'At the moment I just want this one to be healthy, but I think I'd settle for two or three. I really miss helping Rich on the farm, and he's had me on light duties since he found out I was pregnant.'

'It's fair enough.'

'Sometimes I feel so left out. I'm the "little woman" and so I can't go and round up the cattle any more, or drive the tractor, or lug hay bales. Growing a baby is really not that exciting.'

Joss had walked up the corridor to see how they were doing and heard the end of Mindy's snippet. If she was really feeling that way then she would be pleased to have helped out today with bandaging and looking after James and Andy.

'Ahh, the exciting part is still to come,' Melissa said. 'And, remember, it's the stronger sex who get to have the babies. Men just couldn't handle it.'

Joss's lips twitched at Melissa's words, and he figured that although he knew she was probably trying to make Mindy feel better she also had a valid point.

'Lugging hay bales and driving the tractor are easy things. Being a mother—that's a tough job,' Melissa continued.

'Do you have children?'

'No. I haven't had that pleasure yet.'

'Do you want them?'

Melissa sighed. 'More than anything. I would love to be a mother. To care for a family of my own. To nurture them, to provide for them, to be strong for them.' She smiled as she said the last words.

'Well, then, we're going to have to find you a fella. There isn't a shortage in the Outback, so you'll have plenty to choose from—especially in Didja. Heaps of the miners are single. What's your type?'

'My type?' Melissa wasn't really sure about this turn of events.

'What do you like in a guy?'

'Oh.' Melissa thought for a moment, a picture of Joss instantly coming to mind. 'Uh…I'm not really sure. I don't think I've ever consciously sat down and thought about it before.' She thought about Renulf. Initially she'd thought he was her perfect man, but when he'd called off their engagement because he couldn't handle the dedication Melissa had to her work, even though it was that dedication which had brought them together in the first place, she'd realised Renulf really hadn't been. Her perfect man would not only understand her dedication to medicine, but would also understand when she was called out in the middle of the night to deliver a baby. She'd often told Renulf that babies didn't keep office hours, but he still hadn't been able to deal with it.

It had been a lesson for Melissa never to try and date someone outside the medical profession—not unless they were very understanding about the self-sacrifices doctors often had to make. Joss certainly understood that concept. The man had left his family, his life in Perth, and had come to Didja to set up a brilliant medical facility. He would have poured his heart, his soul and a massive chunk of his own time into it. Oh, yes, self-sacrifice was something she instinctively knew Joss Lawson understood one hundred percent.

She pictured him now as she spoke quietly to Mindy. 'I guess I want a man who understands my work—my dedication to it, my need to continue with it. Also, I guess, ultimately I'm looking for a man who'll love me for *me*. For who I am. Faults and all.' As Renulf hadn't been able to do.

'That's what we all want.' Mindy nodded. 'Come on. Be more specific. Just between you and me. What do you like in a man? I like nice hairy legs and big shoulder muscles.'

Melissa smiled. 'Hairy legs, eh?'

'Yep. Rich has a very nice pair. I love running my hands up and down his legs. It makes my hands go all tingly. So, come on. What's your favourite part?'

Melissa thought for a second, remembering how she hadn't been able to stop looking at Joss's legs the first day she'd arrived in Didja. He definitely had a very nice pair of hairy legs too. And then she'd seen his eyes. 'Eyes.' She nodded as she spoke. She remembered the way Joss had looked at her just before he'd kissed her and sighed. 'Nice blue eyes. Deep in colour and very expressive.'

'Blue eyes? Mmm-hmm, what else?'

'Well, all the basics, I guess. Courteous, kind, giving. Not a party animal, but someone who knows how to have a good time—without starting a riot.'

'Oh, goodness. That strikes out half the men in Didja.'

Melissa laughed. 'He needs to have nice hands—clever hands. Healing hands.' She said the last softly.

'Oh, my gosh.' Mindy sat up straighter. 'I know the perfect man for you. It's so simple.'

'A match already? Gee, you're faster than a computer.'

'Joss.' Mindy shrugged, as though it was just so simple. 'Joss would be perfect for you.'

Joss's eyes widened as he listened to what had just transpired. He'd been waiting for a good opportunity to announce his presence but it simply hadn't come, and he hadn't wanted to break up the female bonding session. Mindy thought *he* was ideal for Lis? He swallowed over a sudden lump in his throat.

It might be true that there was an incredible awareness between himself and his new female colleague, but that didn't mean they were going to jump right into a relationship. Physical attraction and need weren't everything in life, and the thought of anything serious, anything permanent, made him break out in a cold sweat.

'Joss?' Melissa closed her eyes for a split second, realising that she had indeed just described Joss when she'd been thinking about what she looked for in a man. What she hadn't expected was for Mindy to pick up on it. She should have been more careful.

'You'd be so perfect for each other. You both have medicine in common as well, which is always a good start. Rich and I had the farm in common. It was what brought us together—that and the confines of the area. Oh, I know.' She clapped her hands, her face lit with excitement. 'You should ask Joss out to dinner.'

'What?'

'Girls can do that nowadays. Equal opportunities and all that. And, secretly, I think the guys love it.'

'They do?'

Mindy giggled. 'Of course. But if you feel uncomfortable making it an actual date, then just ask him to show you around the town, and then you could end up having dinner somewhere.'

She couldn't believe what Mindy was saying, and knew she just wasn't ready for any of this. To date? To ask Joss out to dinner? Sure, she'd enjoyed that kiss. Sure, she was physically attracted to him. But dinner? Just the two of them? That might be moving a little fast, and she was more determined to get to know the people of the town first. Then again, wasn't Joss part of that town?

'We're…uh…both a little busy back in Didja. We have clinics and house-calls and paperwork and you know…general doctoring stuff.'

Joss knew he should move. Knew he was eavesdropping. But he was glued to the spot, unable to believe the conversation going on between the two women. Was this an indication as to whether or not Melissa was really interested in him?

'But that's what makes it so good. He certainly understands the doctoring part, and you do like him, don't you?'

'He's a nice man. Clever, too. But he's my boss.'

Mindy waved away her last words. 'He's also

giving and courteous and all of those other things you listed. Oh, you should totally do this. Go out with Joss. It would be good for him too.'

'What do you mean?'

'Joss has barely dated since he moved to Didja. He's a workaholic and he uses the clinic as an excuse all the time.'

'Perhaps he has his reasons for not dating.'

'Or perhaps he's running away from his problems. Lots of people come to the Outback to do that. I don't really know what happened to him in Perth before he came here. Bub might, she knows everything about everyone, but what I can tell you is that Joss certainly isn't the dating type. You could change all that.'

Melissa emphatically shook her head. 'I don't think so. I may not have come to Didja to run away from my problems, but I have no intention of becoming involved with any man—much less Joss Lawson.' She thought back to the way he'd treated her after that New Year kiss. 'Besides, he's made it crystal-clear that he's not interested in me that way. I've only known him for a short time and he runs hot and cold. He's like a yo-yo so as far as I'm concerned, he's my boss and my colleague and that's it. End of story.'

Mindy sighed and shrugged. 'Well, it was worth a shot.'

Melissa chuckled. 'Come on—we need to finish your check-up. Joss will want to go soon, and I don't want to keep him waiting.

Joss knew she was right. It was the reason he'd come up the corridor in the first place, the carpeted floorboards masking the sound of his footsteps. They needed to get moving. Yet now he seemed unable even to shift his own feet. Had Melissa said what she'd said in order to get Mindy to drop the subject or did she really mean it?

'See? You're already in tune with him. You're thinking like he would think. You have so much in common.' Mindy clapped her hands again as she sat back amongst the pillows so Melissa could measure her stomach.

Melissa sighed. 'Leave it, Mindy.' As she listened to Mindy's heartbeat through the stethoscope, she mentally strengthened her own resolve. She hadn't come to Didja to continue being a people-pleaser. This was her chance at a new start—a new life which she wanted to build with Dex. She wasn't here to continue making the same mistakes as always. She had to be strong, to really put herself first for once. She was in Didja for family—the only remaining family she had.

Melissa put her special baby heart monitor machine onto Mindy's swollen belly and they both listened to the baby's heartbeat.

'Strong and healthy.' Mindy sighed with relief. 'I love hearing that sound.'

Melissa smiled. 'Everything's looking just fine. Keep on doing whatever it is you're doing.'

'Good. I will—and thanks for talking to me. It's so rare that I get real girly-talk time.'

'I've enjoyed it too. Call me any time.' Melissa gave Mindy her mobile number. 'Do mobile phones work out here?'

'Generally they're pretty good.'

As they continued discussing the reception of different mobile network carriers, Joss realised that if he didn't move soon he'd be discovered, and then Lis would know he'd overheard her conversation. Making his feet move, he headed silently back down the corridor.

A minute or two later, the women appeared.

'Ahh, Joss, there you are.'

Did Mindy's tone sound overly bright and cheerful? He decided to ignore it and glanced surreptitiously at Lis. She didn't seem agitated or concerned, and that helped him to relax a little.

'Here I am.' He held his medical kit in his hand and raised an eyebrow at Melissa. 'All done?' Did his tone sound husky? As though he had a secret? Could she see in his face that he'd overheard?

'All done. Are you ready to go?'

'Yes. Andy and James are being driven out to the airstrip. The RFDS should be here in about ten minutes and will complete the transfer. We can check on them once we get back to town later tonight, to review their progress.'

'We don't need to be here to hand over to the RFDS?'

'Not this time. It's all quite straightforward.' He looked at her for a moment and realised she'd been quite looking forward to the transfer part. 'You'll have ample opportunity to meet those crazy flying doctors, but unfortunately today we're on a very tight schedule.'

'Oh, sure. It's no problem.'

'Everything all right with Mindy and the baby?'

'Right as rain,' Melissa replied.

'Well, speaking of rain, that's the reason we need to get moving. There's been a bit of lightning sighted on the horizon.'

Melissa raised her eyebrows. 'Is that bad?'

'It means we don't want to be on a dirt road when the clouds open.' And neither did they want to get trapped in that ute. Together. Just the two of them. No.

'Aww, come on,' Mindy piped up. 'That's when you get a really good mudslide going.'

'And end up wrapped around a tree.'

'Yeah, but only if the tree doesn't move fast enough,' Mindy joked.

Joss grinned. 'Good point.' He nodded to Melissa. 'Let's go.' As they walked out to the front of the property they heard the buzzing sound of the chopper.

'That's Rich.' Mindy clapped her hands. 'Goody. I have so much to tell him.' Her eyes twinkled with delight as she looked from Melissa to Joss and then back again.

'Well, it was a pleasure to meet you,' Melissa rushed in, surprised when the young pregnant woman gave her a hug. It appeared she should get used to being hugged in this town, because the people were most definitely friendly and not backwards in showing their affection.

'It was great. I have a feeling that everything will work out just fine.'

As Mindy waved them off, Joss looked across at Melissa.

'What was that all about? She seemed quite jovial.'

'Oh? Isn't she always like that? You know her better than I do.'

'Not that well. Until Mindy required prenatal care, she was as fit as a fiddle and always had been. Rarely a sick day in her life—well, at least as long as I've known her.'

'I guess she's just relieved that James and Andy are OK, that things weren't worse. Hopefully her husband is returning home with one captured and sedated bull.'

They visited the next few homesteads, trying to get through the necessary check-ups as fast as possible but also not wanting to rush their patients. The emergency with James and Andy had sucked up a lot of time.

The rain started about ten minutes after they

left the second to last homestead, intent on making their way to the Etheringtons—their last port of call for the day. The problem with Outback rain was that when it started it really *started*. Melissa peered out of the windscreen, trying to see something…anything. The wipers were swishing so hard and fast she thought they might wipe themselves right off the car.

'This is bad,' Joss declared a moment later.

Melissa gave him a sidelong glance. Was he talking about the weather, or the tension which existed between them?

'I can't see a thing.'

They were now driving almost at a snail's pace, and she had to agree that visibility was extremely poor. Joss shook his head and steered the car off to the side of the road.

'Won't we get bogged? I mean, it's raining so hard the ground will turn into that mudslide Mindy mentioned.'

'We're in a hard shoulder truck rest-stop. It's usually used for truckers to pull over and catch a few hours' sleep before setting off on the next big drive.'

'What? Even out here in the middle of nowhere?'

'Trucks regularly drive along these roads. Remember—without trucks, Australia stops.'

Melissa couldn't help grinning. 'You sound like an advertising campaign.'

He frowned for a moment. 'I do, don't I?' What had got into him? Why was he trying to make her laugh? Was he trying to impress her in some way? Perhaps it was that overheard conversation which was getting to him. He hadn't liked it at all when she'd described him as a yo-yo, and it was as though he now needed to prove to her that she was wrong.

She'd sounded mortified at Mindy's suggestion of having dinner with him, of going out on a date, and whilst he knew there was a physical attraction on his part—one he wasn't doing too well at controlling right at this moment, given the confines of the ute—he could have sworn, after their shared New Year kiss, that she'd felt that attraction too.

And now he was stuck with the most incredibly beautiful woman he'd ever seen, and when she smiled at him, as she was now, he almost forgot his own name. The woman was driving him to distraction, and he wasn't at all happy about their immediate turn of events.

He flicked on the radio, trying to find something to distract them, but the rain was interfering with the reception and all they managed to pick up was white noise. He turned it off with a final click, plunging them into silence. The engine was off, the radio was off, and all that could be heard was the rain outside. That…and Melissa's breathing.

He tried not to listen, tried not to be aware of the way she breathed in and out. The way her body rose and fell with each breath. He tried not to be aware of the way her sweet, fresh scent was winding itself around him. He tried not to be aware of how stunning she was and how just sitting beside her, the windows fogging up due to their breathing, could make his body overheat. The one situation he'd been trying to avoid all day long had happened, and now he had to deal with it.

'So…' Melissa clicked her fingers. 'What shall we talk about?'

'Uh…' Joss tried not to let the sultry sound of her voice affect him. His mind, which he prided himself on keeping as sharp as a tack, was now completely blank of any suggestions. How was it that this woman could have such an effect on him? A woman who had turned his world upside down and wrenched it inside out even though she didn't know it.

'Usually the weather is the first topic of discussion when making small talk,' she ventured. 'However, I think the weather is the one topic neither of us would like to discuss, given that it has us trapped and sitting in a car.'

'In the middle of nowhere,' he added.

'Yes. So, any ideas? Hobbies? What sort of hobbies do you have?'

'Hobbies?' He pondered the thought for a moment.

'Oh, come on, Joss. Surely you have a hobby—and drinking beer at the pub with your friends doesn't qualify.'

He couldn't help but smile at that. 'Party-pooper.' He thought for another moment, then sadly shook his head. 'The clinic.' He shrugged. 'I guess the clinic is my hobby. It's where I spend most of my free time.'

'That's sad, Josiah.'

'I know. How about you? What are your hobbies?'

'Searching for my brother.'

'But you've found him.'

'Hmm.'

'That's sad, Melissa.'

She looked at him and laughed. It was a mistake. A big mistake. Because in that one second their eyes locked and held.

'You look radiant when you laugh like that.' His words were soft and he shook his head slowly, as though he wished he hadn't said what he had.

'What's going on, Joss?'

He didn't pretend not to understand. 'I don't know.'

'One minute you're nice to me, the next you're—'

'Not so nice,' he finished for her. 'I know.' He reached out and tucked a lock of hair which had come loose from her ponytail back behind her ear. 'I doubt it would help if I said I was confused.'

'I gathered that much.'

Her soft sweet tones only made the fog in his mind more dense. All he could do right now was watch the way her lips moved as she spoke. Those pink, luscious lips which had plagued his dreams. The taste of them, the pressure of them, the need to have them against his own once more. His pride at wanting to show her he wasn't a yo-yo rose to the fore. He was a good man. A catch. One of the most eligible bachelors in town. She should be delighted to have dinner with him. He knew she felt the attraction which existed between them—that strong physical pull which had left them both stunned quite a few times since she'd arrived in town.

She swallowed, noting the intense way he was staring at her. It was as though he knew he was confused but right at the moment didn't care at all. Confusion, right and wrong, the fact that they were colleagues—nothing seemed to matter right at that moment. Nothing except the way he was looking at her.

She told herself she didn't want this—didn't want these feelings she had for him. This wasn't why she'd come to Didja. Then again she reminded herself that she'd vowed to live her life for herself, to put herself first for a while, and right now what she wanted most in the world was to feel Joss's mouth on hers again. To really kiss him this time and not just be teased with the faint, feathering brush of his lips on hers.

'Lis.' He tucked her hair behind her ear again,

this time allowing his hand to linger longer, to caress her cheek.

With her heart pounding wildly against her chest as she saw the look of desire in his eyes, as she watched the movement of his lips as he spoke her name, her lips parted, allowing the pent-up air to escape. She rested her hand on his arm, not sure whether to push him away or to draw him closer.

Indecision warred within each of them, both knowing what they wanted to do but unsure whether they should follow through. That was until she whispered his name and he could resist no longer.

Like lightning, he moved. His hand was at her neck, urging her closer as he leaned towards her. His mouth was crushing down on hers, and both of them were gasping with repressed delight.

CHAPTER SIX

THIS was no soft peck. This was no featherlight brush of his lips on hers. No, this was an intense, fiery and passionate kiss between two people who had been controlling themselves for what seemed like an age rather than just a few days.

It was bizzare to be lip-locked with a man she hardly knew, yet somehow, deep down in her soul, she couldn't deny the feelings he evoked. The heat, the animalistic pleasure, the heady combination of their pheromones mixing together and surging into something so wild and out of control she wondered whether they'd ever be able to tame it.

A guttural moan escaped from him as he tried to bring her as close to him as possible—which was a little difficult with the gearstick in the way. He needed her body pressed hard against his, to feel her soft flesh next to his, needed to feel everything she had to give. Her mouth was so sweet, so flavoursome, so perfect for his own. He focused on eliciting more of a response from her, needing her to be as out of control as he felt.

This was a passion which had been difficult to ignore, and whilst he'd done his best—whilst he'd kept his desire for her repressed, whilst he'd woken the past few mornings from dreams of her—this moment in time was definitely worth it. It was worth it because she made him *feel*.

It had been so long since he'd allowed himself to take such a powerful emotion from someone else, and she was definitely giving him all she had. There was no denying the attraction now. Both of them matched with startling equality the level of passion which flowed freely between them.

It was pleasure and pain. They both knew it was wrong, both knew they shouldn't be doing what they were doing, but the desire had been too strong to ignore, and the look in her eyes and the way her lips had parted…as though they were making themselves ready for him…had all been too much and he'd snapped.

He'd had to have her, and now that he had, now that he knew how incredible it felt to have her mouth against his own, to feel her body against his, he wasn't sure what was supposed to happen next. It had been so incredibly long since he'd held a woman like this, had kissed a woman in such a way, and she was kissing him right back with such abandon it was touching.

Joss loosened his hold on her, but only for a moment. Still it was enough time for her to shift her hands, so she could slide them up his strong firm arm, to feel the muscles beneath the softness of her fingertips. His shoulders were broad, and whilst she moved her mouth against his she traced those sculptured contours, loving the feel of him. When her fingers finally plunged into his hair, ensuring that his head stayed in place, ensuring that his mouth continued to create utter havoc with all of her senses, she moaned with pleasure.

Did he have any idea just how incredible he felt? Did he have any idea just how dynamic it was to have a man appreciate her in such a way? She knew it was only physical, but to be held in such a way, to be kissed in such a way… All of the fantasies she'd had about him honestly hadn't done him justice.

Everything around them seemed to disappear

into oblivion. It was the same as their New Year kiss, when the crowds had all but vanished into thin air, the focus on the two of them intense and mutual. There was no rain. There were no cracks of lightning brightening the sky for a split second. Nothing existed except the two of them, locked together in an embrace so desperate they both wondered if it would ever end.

Both had been hurt in the past. Both found it difficult to trust, to open themselves up again to the possibility of actually having a relationship. None of that mattered here and now, because the temporary emotions of need, of want, of taking, of receiving, of just *feeling* again were all that mattered.

Where she thought the intensity, the passion and the hunger would start to dissipate, after those electrifying first few moments, she found she was mistaken—for his mouth on hers was still demanding a powerful, no-holds-barred response, and she was more than eager to give it.

She was giving it her all, she was one hundred percent involved, and he had to confess he hadn't expected such eagerness from his gorgeous new colleague—not that he was complaining. How could a man possibly complain when he was kissing such a full and sumptuous mouth? When she was driving him crazy with her hands in his hair, holding his head in place, letting him know she didn't want this to end?

Still he needed more. More of her. More feeling. More…Melissa. He was utterly mesmerised by her, and whilst he didn't want to be, at the moment he honestly didn't think he had a choice. His need for her was far too great. Sliding his hand down from her neck, over her shoulder and down, down, to cup the soft underside of her breast, he wondered if he was pushing things just a little too far, too soon. His answer came a nanosecond later, when she moaned with delight and pushed herself further into his touch.

Oh, she was heaven. He hadn't expected any of this, and he was overwhelmed with how she was making him feel. The woman was hypnotic, and he was definitely eager for so much more.

She broke from his mouth, moaning once more with delight, her breathing harsh and uneven. 'Joss.' She whispered his name with such a deep huskiness he was sure she had no idea just how powerful it sounded.

He looked down at her. What little light they

had, due to the black clouds that were blocking the early afternoon sun, was shining onto her face. Her eyes were closed, her lips parted in anticipation of his return, her face turned up to him in wanton rapture.

She was beautiful.

At that thought his eyes widened, and he swallowed. What had he done? He jerked his hand back from where he'd been caressing her breast and put it behind his back. What had he *done*? Her eyelids slowly fluttered open and she looked up at him, her pupils large, her irises deep with delighted emotion. He straightened, pulling away from her.

What had he done?

With his next breath he'd opened the door and stepped from the vehicle into the pouring rain, leaving a shell-shocked, blinking Melissa stupefied.

What had just happened?

She sat staring out at the rain, unsure what had happened and what she was supposed to do about it. He'd just left her, preferring to be out in the rain getting soaked to the skin to being anywhere near her. One second she'd been in his arms, his hands on hers, his mouth on her, both of them caught up in the passion of the moment and the next—nothing.

Melissa crossed her arms over her chest, feeling cold and bereft. Feeling stupid and regretful. Feeling completely insecure. Why had he left? Why had he stopped? Didn't he want her? She shook her head and buried her face in her hands, humiliation washing over her as she recalled the wanton way she'd urged him on.

What was wrong with her? He obviously didn't find her as attractive as she'd initially thought, and once again she was racked with confusion. She'd thought the pull between them had been pretty intense over the past few days, but now she wasn't so sure. In reality, she had to keep reminding herself she knew next to nothing about Joss. He might behave this way with any woman who responded to him.

Then again she recalled Mindy, telling her that Joss didn't date—in which case it could possibly mean that he was attracted to her but didn't want to be. Her mind whirled as she tried to make some sort of sense out of the mess in which she presently found herself.

What the man said and what the man did were two completely different things, and that just made matters worse. She shook her head and pushed her hands through her hair, breathing deeply to stop herself from crying. She was too emotional. She'd become too close to him too quickly, and this was exactly what had happened in her last relationship. She'd misread the signals then and she was doing it again now.

Why had she let herself give in to him? Why hadn't she been more cautious, more careful, more self-controlled?

She jumped fair out of her skin as the driver's door was wrenched open and a dripping wet Joss climbed back into the car. He buckled his seat-belt and started the engine, the whirr of the wind-screen wipers starting immediately.

'It's starting to settle down. Isn't raining as hard as before.' He didn't look at her but instead fiddled with the ute's controls, ensuring the windows were demisted. 'Put your seat-belt on.'

Melissa did as he said, not sure whether she should question his decision to get them back on the road again or not. What about impassable roads? What about mudslides that ended up with the car smashing into a tree? What about keeping them safe?

She glanced over at him and saw that his jaw was firmly set. He was intent on driving them, and nothing she said or did was going to dissuade him. He was obviously a man with a mission to get them out of the middle of nowhere, to get them out of their secluded little environment to somewhere he didn't need to be so close to her. That had to be it. Yo-yo Joss was back with a vengeance, and right now, given her lack of self-control where he was concerned, she was glad he was making the decisions.

Neither of them spoke as he continued to drive the car carefully along the road. Melissa wasn't sure she agreed with him about the amount of rain currently being dumped upon them. It was really as though someone had turned on a tap and—whoosh—the rain came down. It also rammed home the point of how very different things were here in the Outback. Whilst Hobart saw its fair share of rain, being the coldest state in all of Australia, it was nothing compared to this. Out here it was either hot or not. Raining or not. Muggy or not. The four seasons didn't seem to apply at all, and she was amazed that even though it was the same country she'd lived in for all of her life it was completely different from what she was used to.

Finally Joss pulled off the road into a graded gravel driveway which was flooded in certain parts. Again, Melissa was glad of the ute and its four-wheel-drive capabilities. When he brought the ute to a halt, he cut the engine, released his seat-belt and was once more out of the car like a shot.

Melissa shook her head, totally unsure of just how her life had become so complicated so quickly. She stepped out into the cooling rain and headed up the front steps of the large brick homestead before her.

'There you are,' Gemma Etherington said in greeting as she walked towards Melissa.

There were children of various ages around the place, and a moment later, one of the older girls handed her a towel. Melissa looked over to where Joss was just coming in the door, medical bags in tow.

'Hi!' he greeted Gemma warmly, gladly accepting a towel and quickly drying himself off.

'Just leave your wet shoes by the door and come on in,' Gemma called. 'They won't take long to dry. Nothing does in this heat. It may be wet, but it's still hot.' She laughed. 'We were expecting you quite a while ago.'

'Uh…' Joss snuck a sideways glance at Melissa before answering. 'There was an emergency at Murphy's Farm.'

'Oh, we know about that. Mindy called through before the rains hit and told us. I guess you two must have got stuck out there. Are the roads very bad?'

Joss shrugged, making a point not to look at Melissa. He still couldn't believe he'd allowed himself to lose control like that. 'Fair.'

'Ron's over at the neighbours'. I just hope he's going to be able to get home through the dirt roads, otherwise it'll take him a good hour to go around the perimeters on the main roads.'

'He should be fine,' Joss soothed.

Gemma rubbed a possessive hand over her baby bump. 'I hope so. Anyway, come and have something to eat. You both must be starving. Peter,' she said to her son, 'set another two places at the table, please.'

'Righto, Mum.' Peter headed into the kitchen to do as he was asked.

'I'm sorry we're so late,' Joss remarked as he picked up the young three-year-old and started tickling the child's tummy. 'I hope you didn't delay lunch on our account.'

'Not at all. I've been trying to get lunch organised for the past hour and a half, but things do tend to happen, and I learned long ago not to stress about it. We eat when we eat and that's all there is to it.'

Joss smiled. 'You sound like my mum.'

'Well, she would know—having had a large brood of her own. Anyway, I've already had Yolanda make up the guest room, because I don't think this rain is going to abate. We were expecting just Dex, but it's fantastic to get to meet the new doctor.' Gemma smiled widely at Melissa and took one of her hands in hers. 'I didn't think I'd get to meet you until this little one was due to arrive.' She continued to rub her pregnant belly.

'I'm delighted to be here—you have such a wonderful home.' Melissa could really feel the warmth and welcome radiating from this harried mother.

'It's messy, dusty and noisy, but filled with love.'

Gemma let go of her hand as some of the other children started to bring mounds of sandwiches to the dining table. 'All right!' she hollered, clapping her hands to get the attention of her family. 'Go and wash your hands and faces.'

Joss released the squirming three-year-old and held out a chair for Gemma. She sat down, breathing a sigh of relief at being off her feet. Melissa watched her carefully, noting the laboured breathing which took longer than normal to settle.

They were both enveloped into the Etherington household, glad to be able to focus on something other than fighting or ignoring what had happened back in the ute. She noted that Joss seemed relaxed, more so than she'd seen him in Didja, and the way he related to the entire family was quite interesting to see. It was as though this was the real him—the one he only let out on special occasions or in certain circumstances. That definitely intrigued her.

Melissa watched the noisy, happy Etheringtons with delight. All of them were welcoming, and she found no falseness—just genuine friendliness. It hammered home the realisation that this was what she'd been missing throughout her own childhood, this sort of hullabaloo, and it was…enchanting. Whilst she hadn't been lonely as a child, the older she'd grown, the more she'd had the sense that something was missing in her life.

When her parents had died, her heart had been pierced with a grief she hadn't known existed, and with it had come loneliness. It was what had prompted her to search for her birth mother in the first place, and it was also what had prompted her to find Dex.

Yet this…this joyous family simply radiated life. She'd always wanted to have children, but had never thought about how many. First, though, she had to find the right man. Mindy's words, which were still fresh in her mind, made her glance over at Joss. He was laughing with Peter, who appeared to be the eldest of the Etherington children, the two of them joking around with ease and friendliness.

No, Joss Lawson was most definitely not the right man for her. He was too hot and cold for her liking, and whilst he no doubt had his reasons for being that way, unless he decided to face them, to deal with them, there would never be anything between them—despite the physical attraction they obviously felt for each other.

She'd thought she'd found love before with Renulf, but she'd been wrong. Companionship— yes. Deep abiding friendship and a fondness for each other—yes. But not love. Even though they'd met when she'd treated him during one of her rare stints in A&E, he hadn't fully grasped what it would be like to date a doctor. She'd presumed, when he'd proposed to her, that he'd understood, but then—as she'd discovered later—he'd expected her to give up working full-time once they were married. She'd been wrong before, and that meant she could be wrong again.

When they were all sitting around the large dining room table the noise level didn't decrease. Melissa enjoyed the meal very much, but it wasn't the food which had put the smile on her face but the loud rowdiness of the entire clan. They all talked over each other as different topics were discussed. Manners were minded, yet it was one incredibly happy time. This was a real family and the yearning inside her to have this for her very own only intensified.

By the time they'd finished eating it was after

three o'clock and the rain was still pouring down. Gemma went to have a rest while the older kids looked after the younger ones. Joss and Peter brought in their overnight bags from the ute.

'We're staying the night?' she asked Joss. They were standing out on the verandah, which ringed its way around the entire house. He nodded and brushed rain off himself.

'Yes.'

'We're stranded?' She wasn't alarmed, but neither was she pleased. At least, she rational-ised, they didn't need to spend the night on the side of the road in the ute. That would have been... She closed her eyes for a second, not even able to contemplate what might have happened if that had been the case.

Peter heard her comment. 'And what a great family to be stranded with.' He grinned at her, his smile highlighted by the braces on his teeth.

'Oh, I'm not complaining,' she quickly ex-plained. 'Just adapting to the Outback way of doing things.'

Peter carried their bags inside the house, leaving the two of them on the verandah. Melissa put her hands on the railing and looked out at the rain. She heard the door to the house open and close and figured Joss had gone inside, not wanting to be anywhere near her.

She hung her head and shook it. 'Stop thinking about him,' she muttered quietly to herself.

'Probably a good idea.'

Melissa spun around to see Joss standing by the door, hands in the pockets of his almost dry shorts.

'I thought you'd gone inside.' She wasn't going to say anything. She wasn't going to be the one to promote conversation between them—because as far as she was concerned she'd done her fair share of that. He could either talk, be silent, or he could just go. She was through trying to please her colleague, trying to be overly nice and to make sure that he was coping just fine with whatever it was that existed between them. If he didn't want to know, neither did she. If he wanted to forget that dynamic, heart-melting kiss had ever happened, then so would she. If he wanted to be monosyllabic, then so would she.

'I should.'

When he didn't move, she merely shrugged and turned to look at the rain again, effectively dismissing him. He should take the hint. He should leave her in peace. But for some reason he felt compelled to make sure she was all right.

He was still horrified at his weakness earlier, quite unable to believe the powerful hold she had over him. The sight of her parted lips, her eyes filled with desire, her body sending out those 'come hither' signals, and he'd been unable to resist.

And that kiss!

Joss closed his eyes for a moment, still able to taste her, able to breathe in deeply and have her sweet scent envelop him. It was wrong. She was his colleague and he didn't date colleagues. She was business, not pleasure, and he needed to remember that—to keep his distance. He wasn't the type of man to give his trust easily. He wasn't the type of man who could offer a woman like Melissa a bright and happy future. He'd heard her. She wanted a family, lots of children. He wasn't that man. He'd been burned so badly before that he'd learnt his lesson the hard way. Intimacy, giving his heart and his soul to a woman, had ended in such incredible heartache and betrayal that he wasn't fool enough to go there again.

And now they stood—him by the door, her at the railing with her back firmly to him. He wondered what she was thinking, but knew he'd never ask. He wanted to know if she'd been as affected by the kiss as he'd been, but knew he'd never ask. He hoped she'd be willing to help him grow, to help him trust again, but he knew that was definitely one thing he wouldn't ask, no matter how perfect she'd felt in his arms.

She was the only woman since Christina who had made him feel this way, and he was certain that the emotions he felt towards Melissa were growing stronger by the minute, surpassing the ones he'd initially had for his betraying ex-fiancée. If that wasn't warning enough, he didn't know what was.

'Yeah. I should go,' he murmured, and opened the door, going inside to get control over his wayward emotions.

After a moment Melissa turned to make sure he was really gone, before turning her attention back to the rain. 'Hot and cold.' She closed her eyes and tried to forget what had happened back in the ute. The sooner she did that, the better. The sooner she could see Joss Lawson as simply a colleague, the better.

Emotion welled in her throat and a few silent tears rolled down her cheeks. The sooner she realised she was destined to be alone for ever, the better.

CHAPTER SEVEN

THE Etherington family were quite involving, and as the afternoon turned into evening Melissa and Joss found themselves playing all sorts of games with the children. It gave them the space they needed to mentally process what had happened between them, some room to reflect and hopefully to figure out what on earth happened next.

'Dr Jossy!' Bridget, who was five, called to him, demanding his attention for a game of pairs. 'I've laid all the cards out in nice straight lines.' She pointed to her handiwork.

'So I see.'

Melissa watched as Joss crouched down onto the floor, stretching himself out and giving the little girl his undivided attention.

'She's very bossy,' Gemma told Melissa. 'I just hope Joss can handle himself.' The two women smiled.

'I think he has a fair enough chance,' Melissa replied. 'Anyway, whilst everyone's busy, why don't we get your check-up done?'

'Good idea,' Gemma agreed, and after Melissa had collected her medical bag the two women headed into Gemma's bedroom.

'Ron, my husband, says I'm on my feet too much, and he's right—but we have six kids and a farm to run. It's hard *not* to be on your feet all the time.'

'Any problems with the other pregnancies?'

'None. No pre-eclampsia, no gestational diabetes. Nothing.'

Melissa finished taking Gemma's blood pressure, a little concerned at the elevated reading. 'So how does this pregnancy compare?'

'It's different. I can be honest about that. And I have had my own niggling concerns, but that's to be expected, right?'

'That depends on what the niggling concerns are.'

'I've had one or two small bleeds. Sometimes during the night.'

'How long do they last?'

'Less than a minute.'

'Most nights? How many times a week? More than one bleed per night?'

'About three or four times a week, and usually it's two bleeds. They don't come together. They're usually hours apart.'

'Any stabbing pains?'

'Sort of. Sometimes they're more like cramps. Sometimes it's a constant pain which lasts for quite a while.'

'Like Braxton-Hicks?'

Gemma thought for a moment before shaking her head. 'No. Not that bad.'

'Have you been feeling more tired? Any nausea?'

'Mild nausea, but with my girls I had morning sickness the entire pregnancy, so I didn't think that was anything unusual. I'm tired, but I do have a lot going on.'

Melissa listened to Gemma's heart-rate and then the baby's heart-rate. Both were slightly elevated but nothing to cause great concern. 'I'd like you to come to Didja for a few days.'

'What?' Gemma was instantly horrified.

'I need to do some more tests, and I'd like to monitor the baby a little closer. Have you had a scan?'

'No. I only had scans with the first two. Is there really something wrong with my baby?'

'As you said, you have niggling concerns. I share those concerns. I'd like to put both of our niggles to rest.'

Gemma sat up as Melissa packed away her equipment. 'What about Joss? Should we ask his opinion?'

'If you'd like. I realise I'm the new kid in town, and therefore you may think I'm acting a little too cautiously. If you'd prefer Joss to give you a second opinion, we can go and ask him now.'

'You don't mind? You're not offended?'

Melissa smiled and waved Gemma's words away. 'Not at all. You need to be comfortable with your treating doctor and, whilst I may have more experience with these issues, Joss is the doctor you know better.' She left her bag on the floor. 'I'll go get him. Stay here and keep your feet up.'

She found Joss sitting on the lounge, completely at ease, the three youngest children sitting next to him as he held them enraptured with the story he was reading. She watched him for a moment, amazed at how wonderful he was with the children. When he looked up and saw her standing there, he quirked an eyebrow. 'Problem?'

He looked gorgeous, carefree and downright sexy. It took her a moment to make her mind work, as seeing him like this had completely wiped all rational and coherent thought from her.

'Uh…I need you to…' She jerked her thumb over her shoulder. 'Uh…' Come on, Melissa. Concentrate. She closed her eyes, blocking out the sight of him. 'I need you to come and check Gemma.'

His expression instantly changed to one of concern. Not wanting to alarm the children, he shifted them slowly, calling over Yolanda, the oldest girl, to finish reading to them.

'What's wrong?' he asked quietly as they headed towards Gemma's bedroom.

Joss stopped off in the bathroom to wash his hands, all the while listening to what Melissa had to say. 'Care to guess a diagnosis?'

She shook her head. 'I need to do tests. Bloods. Amniocentesis and ultrasound to begin with.'

'OK. No hunches?'

'Ante-partum haemorrhage?' She shrugged. 'She told me she's had a few small bleeds, and with the pains…' She shook her head. 'Or I could be wrong. I need to do tests. Too many possibilities.'

'How elevated is the baby's heart-rate?'

'It's up, but not on the dangerous scale.'

'Not yet. Right.' He walked purposefully into Gemma's room and proceeded with a thorough check-up. When he was finished, he looked his patient carefully in the eyes. 'I have to say that I agree with Lis on this one, Gem. Your other pregnancies weren't like this, and as you've had quite a few to compare it to that's the biggest factor to indicate there may be something wrong.'

Gemma rubbed her stomach lovingly. She was only twenty weeks, but was well and truly showing.

'We'll contact the Royal Flying Doctor Service and get you airlifted to Didja tomorrow morning.'

'That soon?' Gemma was shocked. 'But the kids and—'

'I'll get Peter to find Ron,' Joss said. 'He should be here.'

'He'll be on his way home now,' Gemma told him, then shook her head. 'Tomorrow morning?'

'The sooner we find out what's going on, the

better,' Melissa encouraged. 'Your health and the baby's health are paramount.'

'But what about the rest of my kids? My family?' Her voice broke on the word and Melissa felt her pain. To have all this—such love and happiness—and to leave it even for a short time would be painful.

Tears sprang to the woman's eyes as a moment later her husband walked into the room.

'Perfect timing. I was just about to go and contact you,' Joss said as Ron rushed to his wife's side.

'What's wrong? What's going on?'

Joss and Melissa explained the situation as Ron held his wife, comforting her in such a loving way.

'Tomorrow? So soon?'

'The sooner we start on the tests, the sooner we'll—' Melissa began but he waved her words away.

'You're right. You're right. It's fine. It'll be OK. Everything will be OK. You'll see. We'll cope,' Ron quickly assured Gemma. 'We've raised all of our children to be self-sufficient, and Peter's almost seventeen now. He's the oldest, and he's more than capable of taking control of things.'

Joss looked over at Melissa and saw such empathy in her face that he couldn't help but be moved by it. She genuinely cared about her patients, she was really empathising with them, and it showed him what a good doctor she truly was. It also showed him a lot about the person she really was. He doubted Christina would ever have given people in distress another thought other than how their own distress might affect her.

He was about to look away when she turned and met his gaze. They stared at each other for a long moment, and he could see her pain at splitting up this family, but the fact remained that Gemma needed to go to Didja for tests. Joss inclined his head towards the doorway, indicating they should give Ron and Gemma some privacy.

She nodded, and together they headed out and down the corridor. Once there, she expected Joss to go in a different direction, to leave her to her own devices, but instead he held the front door open and waited for her to go out before him.

'Best to make ourselves scarce for a few minutes. Ron and Gemma will want to talk to the kids.'

She nodded, surprised at his forethought. 'They're a very open and loving family.'

'They are.'

'You were brilliant with those children. All of them were so enraptured by what you were reading.' Melissa stood at the verandah railing, looking out at the never-ceasing rain. Joss perched himself against the far railing, ensuring there was quite a bit of distance between them. 'And you're completely natural with the older children as well,' she praised.

He shrugged. 'I have siblings. Five of them, to be precise.'

'Really? I didn't know that. But then, there's a lot about you I don't know.' It explained why he was being so chatty all of a sudden. Being here with the Etheringtons reminded him of being with his own family, and that had to inspire a certain sort of comfort in him.

He shrugged those broad, firm shoulders of his and crossed his arms over his chest. 'I guess I'm used to dealing with children, family situations and the like. You know—taking responsibility, helping out, reading stories, giving orders. Coming here to the Etheringtons' is like walking into my own home. In fact, the last time I was here I offered to help Peter do the dishes and we sort of ended up having a soapsud fight in the kitchen. Gemma got cross with both of us.'

Melissa couldn't help but laugh. 'I can imagine.' It appeared Joss was having one of his 'hot' phases, and she liked it. Of course as he was now running hot it would mean that a cold snap would no doubt come later, but she decided that for now she'd go with it. What could it hurt? He obviously had good reasons for being the way he was. Maybe, just maybe, there was something she could do to help him.

'But we cleaned the place up. Even mopped the floor.'

'I should think so—I'm sure you made your mother proud.'

His grin was wide, his face relaxed as he spoke again. It made him look more handsome than usual. 'I used to have soapsud fights with my brothers all the time. In fact on one occasion the kitchen floor was so wet that when my brother Tony lunged for me, I slipped, fell and cracked my head on the corner of the kitchen cupboards as I came crashing down.' He pointed to the side of his head. 'Four stitches.'

Melissa laughed. 'I'll bet your mother was impressed! How old were you?'

'About Peter's age.'

'So, you're the oldest?'

'I am.'

'Must have been fun?'

He shrugged. 'I guess. I don't know any different, so I can't really comment. We had noisy dinners, talked over each other.'

'Sounds amazing.'

'But there was always some job or other that needed doing. Always.'

'Especially as you were the oldest, eh?'

'Exactly.'

'Well, if it helps any, there were always jobs that needed doing at *my* house, and I was the only one there to do them.'

'I guess it doesn't matter whether you're in a brood or an only child—there will always be jobs to do.'

She smiled. 'And when you become an adult those jobs are endless.' Melissa sighed and looked out into the rain, rather than looking at him. He was so very nice when he was like this, all relaxed and talkative. She liked this Joss much better than the broody one—the only problem being that this one was harder to resist. However, resist she would. She didn't want to risk misreading the signals again. 'Do you have any idea just how lucky you are to have such a big family?'

'I do. I didn't for quite a while, but when I decided to move to Didja they were one hundred percent behind me. All of them.'

'You're close?'

'Yes. We usually try and get together once or twice a year.'

'That's nice. Family's important.'

It was darker now, the sun having been pushed out by the clouds, yet still she could see the outline of his silhouette as he half-leaned, half-sat against the railing, his arms still crossed firmly over his chest. They were both silent for a while, just absorbing and listening to the sounds of the Outback, but for the first time their silence wasn't the uncomfortable kind.

'I guess it must be hard for you. Being alone, I mean.'

'That's why I like to surround myself with interesting people.'

'What were your parents like?' Joss asked, liking the fact that they seemed to be having a normal and casual conversation. She was a colleague. This was business. He was finding out a bit more about his employee.

She instantly smiled, and his gut clenched as she looked his way. She had the most amazing smile. He firmed his jaw, fighting back the attraction.

'They were sweet. Loving. Kind. Caring. The things parents usually are. They were both only children, and though they wanted a large brood of their own it simply never happened. They were in their late forties when they adopted me, and even then they only got me because I was so much older than the babies who were being put up for adoption. They didn't care, though. They just wanted someone of their own to love.'

'And your biological mother? No family on her side?'

'Eva? Not that she knew of. Her parents had both died, as had her older brother.'

'I guess I can understand why getting to know Dex is so important to you. He's a good guy.'

'Who does rain dances.'

Joss chuckled and swept a hand out at the rain surrounding them. 'And they work.' He slowly shook his head. 'Typical Dex.'

'I did read that people in the Outback can go quite insane when a drought breaks. Perhaps Dex goes insane before that?'

He shook his head. 'But the drought isn't broken yet. This is just good drenching rain.'

'Oh. So we can only blame Dex for good drenching rain?'

His eyes lit with laughter. 'Afraid so.'

'Dex sounds like fun.' Her words were quiet, intense.

'He's a good mate,' Joss agreed. 'A little insane at times, but good fun nevertheless.'

'Insane. I like that. The insanity plea always works well in court—not that I'm suggesting we take him to court for being a little insane. I'm just…well…I'm babbling.' Melissa looked at Joss a little closer. 'Are you all right? You're looking a little pale.' Was she about to get the return of the Ice Man?

The humour had drained from his face, because he knew all about court cases—especially on a personal level—and he knew just how 'insane' they could get. 'I'm fine.'

'Sorry, Joss. I was only joking about Dex. I don't really think he's insane.'

'Sure.' He tipped his head back and closed his eyes.

'Want to talk about it?' she ventured, unsure of what sort of response she'd get. Would it be hot or cold?

'What?'

He looked at her, a scowl on his face. Melissa swallowed, and then took a deep breath before plunging ahead. 'Do you want to talk about whatever it is that's bothering you?'

'Nothing's bothering me.'

She held up her hands in surrender. 'Good. Fine. Sorry. I must have grasped the wrong end of the stick.' The Ice Man had returned. Well, it had been nice while it lasted, and she'd certainly discovered a bit more about the man she hadn't been able to stop thinking about. 'I guess I'll head in. I can hibernate in the spare room if Gemma and Ron are still talking to their children.'

She took a few steps towards the door, the automatic sensor light coming on, blinding her for a moment. Joss called her name and she turned to look at him. He was so gorgeous, leaning against the railing, arms still crossed, the rain behind him framing him to perfection.

'Don't go on my account. You stay here. I'll go.'

'What? You're going to storm out into the rain again just to get away from me?'

Joss raked a hand through his hair at her words, deciding that he probably deserved them. 'You know, Lis, you're not at all what I expected.'

'What did you expect?'

'I don't know, but not this.'

'Do you often find being around women difficult?'

'Yes. Er…no. That's not what I meant.'

'Then what *did* you mean, Joss?' She wasn't angry with him, but she was becoming increasingly frustrated. 'I've been trying for days to figure you out, and all I keep doing is going around in circles.'

'Why do you need to figure me out?'

'So I can cope working alongside you. So I can work harder at ignoring this pull I feel towards you. So I can get on with my life, which isn't supposed to be this complicated.'

'Look—' he ground out, taking a few angry steps forward but stopping before he got too close to her. Being close to Melissa wasn't a good thing, especially when she had the appearance of an angel, framed beneath the artificial light. 'I don't do dating. I don't do relationships. It's just the way it is. I was betrayed four years ago by the woman I was going to marry and I vowed then never to trust another. Something happened—something which wasn't my fault. The press had a field day with it. Dex, my closest friends, and of course my family stood by—me but Christina…' He shook his head, bitterness in his tone. 'She not only believed the lie, she helped to fuel it. Right when I needed her most.'

Melissa could feel the pain and betrayal radiating from him and her heart empathised, but she was sure he didn't want it. 'I understand about not being able to trust. I understand about feeling betrayed. For years I wondered why my mother had given me up for adoption. Why didn't she want me? I guess it's the sort of question all adopted children ask themselves. And then, when I finally got my answer, I was actually grateful that she'd given me up. You see, she hadn't trusted herself with Dex or myself, fearing she might actually harm us. It was a brave decision to make, given she was so manically depressed.'

'So you forgave her?'

'Of course. If I hadn't, I might still be walking around bitter and empty, trying to fill that void with numerous relationships, not being able to come out on house-calls for fear of seeing happy families living in harmony together. I think that's why Dex probably hates doing house-calls.'

Joss pondered her words for a moment, his anger dissipating a little. 'That's quite an insight. Quite spot-on, too. I actually hadn't thought of it like that before—why he is the way he is.' He was quiet for a moment, then asked, 'Do you still have a void?'

'I'm here, aren't I? I've tried to fill it—oh, in so many different ways. I've looked for love and acceptance in many places, but after my engagement ended—after yet another setback and someone else not wanting me—I realised I was looking in all the wrong places.'

'Hence why you're here?'

'Well, yes—but also no. You see, I needed to

find that acceptance within myself first. I needed to accept that Renulf didn't want to marry me because I simply wasn't what he needed—not any more. It was different when we first met—it always is different in the beginning—and then, as time went on…' She shrugged as she trailed off. 'The point is, I'm still trying to like *me*. I'm a work in progress.'

'So you don't have time for relationships and things like that either?'

'No.'

'Hmm.'

They were silent again, and whilst she willed him to say more, he didn't, and she started to feel completely stupid standing in the middle of the verandah beneath the light. Without another word, she turned on her heel and left—and this time he didn't try to stop her.

CHAPTER EIGHT

AFTER dinner, things settled down quickly. The younger ones were bathed by Yolanda, and Peter checked their teeth. Ron, their father, read them bedtime stories before tucking them in. The older children stayed up talking quietly for a while, before heading off to their rooms. Melissa and Joss kept their distance from each other the entire time, neither quite sure what to do or say next.

'Do you know where you're sleeping?' Joss asked.

Melissa shook her head. 'Where are you sleeping?'

'Out here on the sofabed.'

'Oh.'

'Here. I'll show you where to go. I think Peter's already put your overnight bag into the guest room.'

'I was wondering where it was.'

Melissa noticed both she and Joss were being extra polite with each other, careful and particular, and trying desperately not to say anything personal.

They bumped into Peter in the hallway.

'How are you holding up with the news about your mum? Everything all right?' Joss asked the boy.

Peter shrugged in the nonchalant way teenagers did when they tried to pretend nothing was really bothering them. 'Mum has to go to hospital. It happens. It means more chores for everyone, which none of us like—especially me, as most of them will become my responsibility.'

Joss chuckled. 'Spoken like a true eldest child.' He clapped the boy on the back. 'You'll do fine. I was just showing Melissa to her room.'

He nodded. 'Bathroom's directly opposite your room—the girls' bathroom. Toby, Lee and I share the lower bathroom. Yolanda, Selena and Bridget share that one.' He pointed up the hallway. 'Mum and Dad get their own *en suite*.' He sounded as though that wasn't fair at all.

'Hey. When I was at home, all eight of us had to share one bathroom. At least you have three in this house.'

Peter rolled his eyes. 'I don't even want to go there. Eight people? One bathroom?' He shuddered. 'Total torture. Anyway—night.' He shuffled off down the hallway, and within the next instant they were left alone…again. Awkwardness filled the space between them as they both tried not to be so aware of each other.

Melissa jerked a thumb at the door behind her. 'This is where I'm sleeping?'

'Yes. Yes. That's the spare room.' Joss shoved his hands into his pockets, hoping at least this way he'd keep from hauling her into his arms and kissing her goodnight—which was exactly what he wanted to do.

'And you'll be on the sofabed?' She edged back and reached for the door handle.

'Yes. I've slept on it before. It's quite comfortable.'

'Good. Good.'

Silence.

Melissa racked her brain for something to say, but the more she searched the less she found. It was his nearness combined with his spicy scent which was turning her mind to mush. They were close, but not too close. Far, but not too far.

Indecision. Confusion. Stress. They were all making an appearance. Heat. Need. Desire. Combine everything together and it was no wonder the tension between them could have been sliced with a scalpel.

'Well…' Joss eased back, taking a step down the hallway—because it would be all too easy to simply step forward and press his lips to hers. 'I guess I'll go check on Gemma before I turn in.'

'Oh, that's OK. I can do it,' Melissa offered quickly, eager for him to be down at the other end of the house before she tried to make sense of the emotions she was experiencing. 'I'm closer— geographically speaking.' She pointed to Gemma and Ron's room, just up from her own. 'You go get your bed set up.'

Joss shrugged. It was an out and he'd take it. 'OK, then.' Another step away. 'I guess I'll see you in the morning, then.'

'I guess you will.' Her eyes held his. Neither of them looked away. Both of them seemed to be speaking volumes, but nothing was actually said. It wouldn't take much to step forward and press her lips to his once more, and when his gaze momentarily dipped to look at her own mouth she almost faltered. Leaning back, she flattened herself against the door, wanting him to go before she really lost control.

'All right. Sleep well.'

'You too.'

Sighing, she watched him turn and walk down the hallway, back towards the living room. He had such a nice back, such a nice walk…such a nice butt. After another soulful sigh, she went into the spare room.

Her medical kit was on the bed beside her overnight bag, but she ignored it for a moment. She sat down, her whole body shaking slightly. The man was going to drive her to distraction if she wasn't careful, so careful she must be. Focusing on work would most definitely help, and after she'd taken a few deep breaths, relaxing her tense muscles, Melissa gathered the items she would need for Gemma's check-up and made her way back out to the hallway.

She knocked on the master bedroom door and heard Gemma call, 'Come in.'

Melissa went in and was pleased to find Gemma in bed, lying on her side, surrounded by pillows.

'It's already taking me ages to find a comfortable

position and I'm only in the middle of the pregnancy!' Gemma complained, but not in a bad way.

Melissa smiled and knelt down beside her patient. 'I just need to check you over once more, and then I'll leave you in peace to get some sleep.' Melissa wound the blood pressure cuff around Gemma's arm and was pleased with the result. 'It's lower than before, so the rest is definitely doing the two of you good.'

Ron came into the bedroom from the *en suite* bathroom. 'How's my girl doing?'

'Better than before.' She listened to both Gemma's heart and then the baby's. Ron and Gemma shared a special moment as they too listened to the baby's heartbeat.

'It sounds so healthy.'

'It's good, but it's still a little fast.' Melissa knelt on the floor and started packing up her equipment as she spoke. 'After we've run some tests it may turn out that what you need to do is rest for the remainder of your pregnancy. Now, I know that will be difficult—but it's a must. It would be ideal for you to remain here, rather than being hospitalised—which is what we want to avoid. Separating you from your family for any extended period of time won't be good for you, but if that's what has to happen in the end, then—'

'That's what has to happen,' Gemma finished, and nodded. 'It's the first pregnancy I haven't been able to carry on through. I've even had four of them delivered right here at home, and everything has always been fine. I just don't understand what's happening.'

'And that's why we need you to go to Didja tomorrow. The sooner we find out what's really going on, the better.'

Gemma nodded. 'I know. It's all just come as a bit of a shock.'

Melissa stood, bag in hand. 'I'll leave you both to get some sleep, but if anything goes wrong tonight, if you have a bleed or any pain, you send Ron to get either myself or Joss or both. Understand? We *want* you to wake us up. Don't be considerate and let us sleep. OK?'

'Right. Be inconsiderate to the house-guests. Got it.' Gemma smiled. Melissa turned and headed for the door before Gemma called her name. 'Oh, and thanks.'

Melissa smiled warmly. 'My pleasure. Goodnight and sleep soundly.'

Joss heard her call goodnight to Gemma and Ron and then head back into her room. He lay down on the sofabed, hands behind his head, and stared up at the ceiling fan whirring softly around. The rain hadn't necessarily cooled everything down. In fact, it had made this room more humid than before. Or perhaps that was just him— sweating under the realisation that it had been so incredibly difficult not to kiss Melissa goodnight.

Had she been waiting for him to do it? Had she wanted him to do it? Was she upset that he hadn't? He closed his eyes for a moment. He had no idea where he stood, and he wasn't a man who liked to be unsure of his footing.

A female doctor. That was all he'd wanted for the clinic. It had been top of his priority list. A female doctor for the female population of Didja and its surrounding communities. When he'd learned that Dex's sister had wanted to get to know her brother and that she was a qualified OB/GYN he hadn't been about to look a gift horse in the mouth. What he simply hadn't counted on was the way he'd feel so protective towards her.

Of course he'd told himself it was because he

wanted to make sure she concentrated on her job here, that she didn't get side-tracked with thoughts of romance and marriage. She was here for twelve months to do a job and to get to know her brother. That was all. So why had he been so incredibly possessive of her—especially when they'd gone to the mining headquarters and Scott the Sleaze had tried to put his moves on her? It was all quite puzzling, as Joss had never been the possessive type in the past.

Still, here he was, not only feeling possessive towards his colleague but wanting to kiss her again and again. It wasn't right. It wasn't professional. Slowly he acknowledged the truth of the matter—he didn't want anyone else to have her because he wanted her all for himself.

It was wrong. So wrong. And yet when they were close, when he held her, it was so incredibly right.

When he'd initially come to Didja he'd been hurting, trying to get his life back on track. The community had rallied around their new doctor and had certainly made him feel welcome, but there was one thing he'd realised: when it came to having personal relationships in small towns everyone knew everything and everyone. If he'd dated at all, he would have been under close scrutiny—and he'd already had his fair share of that back in Perth.

To be accused of medical negligence at a big city hospital, to have it plastered all over the media and then to be privately told that he was being offered as a sacrificial lamb by the head of the hospital had been tough. He'd lost his faith in the system—not only the hospital hierarchy but also the political leaders. At least here in Didja *he* was the boss. He ran the clinic the way a clinic should be run, with truth, honesty and integrity, and he wouldn't be made the scapegoat for any political games. Not ever again.

When the whole state, from your patients to the hospital board to the members of parliament, all thought you were some sort of 'Doctor Death'; when your fiancée—the woman who was supposed to love you—went to the press telling lies about your personal relationship and painting you to be some sort of monster; when you went from being an upstanding member of society to being threatened with jail time, the last thing you wanted was to move to a new place for a fresh start and be once more under close scrutiny. That was how Joss had felt.

That was why he'd tried to keep to himself in the beginning—until the good people of Didja had decided to bring the pub to his house and *really* welcome him to town. Still, as far as romantic relationships went it would be impossible for the whole town *not* to become involved. But he'd been hurt on so many levels before, and for four years he'd managed to keep that part of his heart locked securely away.

Until Melissa.

He wasn't the type of man who could just hand over his heart, give over his trust, open up all aspects of his being and love a woman unconditionally. Was he?

He thought about Christina, and the emotional trauma she'd put him through when he'd needed it the least. He couldn't put his heart out there again and risk it getting cut into tiny little pieces before being pulverised, then liquefied, and then tipped into the sewer.

He knew Melissa wasn't Christina, and that so far, in the short time he'd known her, she'd displayed qualities such as loyalty, generosity and integrity, but he'd been duped before and he wasn't about to be duped again.

People could change. Could *he* change? Could he open his heart to the beautiful blonde woman who was just up the corridor from him? The woman who felt so right in his arms, who kissed like an absolute dream, who listened and really seemed to be interested in him? Was he strong enough to take the chance?

Joss closed his eyes, pain and indecision piercing his chest. What if she hurt him? What if she didn't? What if what they felt for each other was not only more than an initial attraction but the real deal? What if he was being given a second chance at happiness, at friendship, at love? He'd always wanted to get married, to have children of his own, but after Christina's betrayal he'd figured that would never happen—that he'd never love another woman as much, nor would he ever trust another again.

Was Melissa his second chance? Was she worth the risk?

Melissa quickly got ready for bed, padding across to the bathroom to do her teeth before quietly settling down beneath the ceiling fan, a cotton sheet draped over her. The rain was still pattering, lightly now, outside the open window. Here she was, in the middle of the Outback, in the middle of nowhere, in a complete stranger's house and she'd never felt safer.

She knew it wasn't just because the Etheringtons had been so caring and welcoming. She knew it wasn't because the Outback was a place of untamed beauty with not one scrap of artifice. No, she felt completely safe due to the man who now slept on the fold-out sofabed in the front living room of this old homestead.

Her life had certainly changed quite a bit since arriving in Didja. The question was, was it all for the better? Was getting involved with Joss enhancing her life? All she knew was that it was definitely confusing it.

All she wanted was a man who would hold her, kiss her, want to be near her. She wanted her life to be like the Etheringtons'—to have a home, a husband, children of her own. Uncles and aunts to come and visit, bringing their own children along so the house dissolved into a mass of noise, laughter and love.

Over the years she'd invested so much of herself in relationships with others, whether it was as a loving daughter or in a more romantic way, such as the relationship she'd shared with Renulf. And yet time after time things had gone wrong. Something had always happened to change those relationships and she'd be left all alone. Again.

If it wasn't one thing it was another, and this time around she wondered whether she was getting ready to tread on that pond of thin ice again. Letting herself stay too long in a fairytale world where everything turned out right would only end up with her getting hurt—possibly hurting both of them—and that was the last thing either of them needed.

Melissa awoke the next morning to the faint buzzing of an aeroplane. She opened her eyes, unsure for a moment where she was. Then she heard high-pitched giggling and the patter of little feet down the hallway, followed by big thumping footsteps as a deeper voice growled.

She sat up in bed, remembering where she was and why she was there. The plane was sounding closer—the RFDS plane—and she glared at the clock.

'Eight-thirty!' Flicking back the cool cotton sheet, she quickly pulled a change of clothes from her bag and dressed, mortified that she'd slept so late. She had no doubt it was because she'd tossed and turned for half the night, her mind filled with indecision about what she needed to do.

She tidied the room and gathered her bags together before opening the door, then quickly stepped back as she narrowly missed being run down by a three-year-old and a five-year-old, running past her door squealing.

What surprised her even more was Joss, who was growling as he chased after them. He stopped when he saw her, straightening from his hunched-over position, and smiled in that adorable way which simply melted her heart.

'Morning.'

'Hi. I see you're…uh…busy.'

'Yep. The RFDS plane is just arriving, and Ron's driven out to greet them. Looks as though you'll get to meet the crew today.'

'Good. Right.' Work. Talking about work

was a neutral way to start the day. 'I'll go check on Gemma.'

'She's resting out on the verandah,' he supplied, trying not to visually caress the woman before him. Melissa looked delectable first thing in the morning, her hair loose and gorgeous as it floated around her shoulders. It was an image he knew would stay with him for ever.

'Good. It seems she made it through the night with no complications. That's another good sign.'

'Actually, she did have a pain.'

'What?'

'About an hour ago. But as you were sleeping and I was already awake Ron came and got me to check on her. Everything was fine,' he rushed on, seeing the concern on Melissa's face. 'The baby's heart-rate; Gemma's blood pressure. No swelling. No bleeding. Everything's fine,' he reiterated.

'Right. Good. Thanks.' She paused for a moment and pushed a hand through her hair, wishing she'd been able to find her hairband so she could put it back. 'You could have woken me, you know.'

Joss had been so mesmerised by her actions, by the gorgeous blonde strands glinting in the sunlight, that he'd momentarily tuned out from what she'd been saying. 'Oh. Yeah.' He waved her words away. 'It's OK. It was no big deal. To let you sleep, I mean. It's going to be a long day.'

'It is?' Melissa put her overnight bag down and pushed her hands into the pockets of the three-quarter-length jeans she'd packed, her cotton shirt falling over the waistband. 'Listen, I've been thinking.'

'Always a good start to the day,' he replied, and she couldn't help but smile. Joss stared. Why had she done that? Why had he provoked such a smile? She was beautiful. Completely and utterly breathtakingly beautiful first thing in the morning. Her lips were redder, her eyes were richer, and her hair was so glorious he was hard pressed not to reach out and sift his fingers through the silken strands.

'Uh…I think it might be better if I go back on the plane with Gemma. That way she has immediate and constant care. I'm not suggesting,' she quickly rushed on, 'that the RFDS aren't capable of providing such care. It's just that—'

'It's a good idea.' Joss nodded. 'I was thinking along the same lines.' Mostly because of

Gemma's health, but also because he wasn't sure he could handle a three-hour drive back to town with Melissa sitting so close beside him and be able to keep his hands to himself.

'You were?' Did he want to get rid of her? Was it for Gemma's sake he wanted her out of his ute for the drive back to Didja, or was it because of the repressed sexual tension which was palpable between them? 'I mean. Good. That's good. Good we're both on the same page.'

'Patient's health comes first,' he agreed. 'Plus, it's also a good way for you to get to know Phemie. She's one of the main RFDS doctors employed in this district.'

'Phemie?'

'Short for Euphemia.'

Melissa smiled again, but this time it was more relaxed. 'Great name.'

'Great woman.' He stood there, staring at her, watching her every move, wanting to plant his mouth over hers more with each passing second. Did she have any idea how beau—? No. He cut the thought off. He couldn't think like that. He needed to find a way to put some distance between them, and also find a way to stop wanting a repeat of yesterday afternoon, when she'd let him kiss her.

Joss felt a tugging at his shorts and looked down at Bridget. 'Hello.'

'Come on, Dr Jossy,' said the five-year-old. 'You're the growly ogre chasing the princess and the prince through the forest.'

'Yeah. Come on,' three-year-old Lee chimed in.

'Best get to it, then.' Melissa picked up her bag again.

Joss's answer to his little friends was to assume his hunched-over 'growly ogre' position, and the two children ran away squealing with delight. Joss instantly straightened again. 'That should hold them for a moment.'

'I'd best go check on Gemma. Make sure she's ready for this transfer.' Melissa took a step away, but was stopped when Joss placed a hand on her arm.

'Wait a second.' He dropped his hand, as though the touch had burnt him. The itch to touch her hair was becoming overwhelming. 'Lis?'

'Yeah?' Her heart-rate had started to increase at the way he was looking at her.

'I'm…um…' He stopped and breathed out,

staring at her loose blonde hair. He couldn't resist her any longer and reached out to touch the silken locks. 'Glorious,' he whispered. 'The colour, the feel of it. So soft and silky.'

Melissa parted her lips at his touch, unable to believe how incredibly intimate it was to feel his fingers in her hair. 'Joss?' His name was a breathless whisper.

'Hmm?' He swallowed, and then, as though realising what he was doing, he instantly dropped his hand and moved back. 'Oh, gosh, Lis. I'm sorry.' He closed his eyes for a second before looking at her once more.

'I need to tell you that I'm not sorry about yesterday, but that doesn't mean it can happen again…and again,' he rushed on. 'Even though we might want it to.'

She dragged a breath in and slowly let it out, desperate to control her mounting heart-rate. 'Agreed. Yes. You're right. We're colleagues.'

'Yes, we are.'

'We both have plans. Things to achieve.'

'Yes,' he agreed again.

'I didn't come to town looking for…' She put her bag down again and indicated the space between them. 'For this.' Or to feel how amazing it was to have him touch her hair, or her shoulder, or to hold her hand, or to gather her firmly to his body. She hadn't come here looking for any of that.

'You came to get to know your brother.'

'Exactly. That's what I need to focus on. That and getting to know the people of this community.'

'Yes.' Part of him wanted to point out that *he* was part of the community, and that *he* wouldn't be averse to getting to know her a lot better. Thankfully, he was able to refrain. He had to keep his distance for both their sakes.

'Dex. I need to focus on getting to know Dex. He's important to me.'

'And so he should be. I do understand where you're coming from, Lis.'

'Good.' She breathed a sigh of relief. 'That's good.'

'Yes, it is. It's very good,' he agreed, knowing they both not only sounded like fools but were probably lying to themselves. But taking a step back, a very big step away from the turbulent emotions of yesterday, from the way she'd felt so perfect in his arms, was most definitely the right thing to do.

'I'm glad we had this chat.'

'So am I.'

They were both running, both hiding beneath the nearest table, locking their hearts up tight, unable to take the risk. At least not just yet.

'Good. Well…you drive safe now. You hear?'

'I will.'

'I'd best go find Gemma.'

'Yes.'

And with that she turned and walked away from him.

CHAPTER NINE

Two days after she was admitted to the Didja hospital Gemma was airlifted back home by the RFDS. Melissa had performed the tests, done the scans and come to the conclusion that it was an ante-partum haemorrhage—as she'd first suspected.

'One of the blood vessels which takes food to the baby isn't working too well. What we can do, however, is give you daily injections and monitor you. That way the baby will receive what it needs to grow, and also you'll be able to stay home. Complete bed-rest, though.' Melissa had been stern.

Thankfully, Rajene, the woman who had helped deliver Gemma's last four children, had come to the hospital to visit Gemma, and Melissa had discovered that Rajene, who was almost seventy-five years old, had trained as a midwife in an island country called Tarparnii. Whilst she held no official qualifications in Australia, she was more than capable—and close enough in distance—of giving Gemma the daily care required. Joss had confirmed that he trusted Rajene, and that she was indeed a very good midwife, so Melissa's initial fears were calmed.

'I will make sure she does not do too much. I will help her. You shall see. This babe will be as strong as the others,' Rajene promised.

'I have no doubt.'

During the following week Rajene called Melissa on a daily basis to report on Gemma's condition.

'She is behaving well and very much resting. We are all so proud. Peter and Yolanda are doing marvellous with the helping. Gemma stays in her bed or on the sofabed. Blood pressure has improved to normal levels, the babe's signs are good, and there has been no more bleeding.'

It was much the same as Rajene had reported the day before, but this was the type of good news Melissa didn't mind hearing again and again. 'Good to hear. Thank you, Rajene.'

As she put the phone down, she reflected on

her first full week in Didja. It had been mostly good, with the people of the community still continuing to welcome her. She'd visited the pub a few nights, but on others had preferred simply to unwind in her apartment.

On those nights she would lie on her bed beneath the ceiling fan, trying to get cool and pretending to read a book, whilst all the time she'd listen for noises coming from Joss's apartment next door. She'd learned that his apartment was a mirror image of her own, which meant that their bedroom walls were a shared wall. It was strange to think that when she put her hand up to the wall he was on the other side. Sleeping. In his bed. Probably wearing next to nothing.

She closed her eyes, trying to school her thoughts. She was in the middle of a clinic and she was once more thinking about her boss. This wasn't professional behaviour at all, and she knew she needed to conquer the emotions Joss continually evoked within her.

Melissa had been as jittery as a cat on a hot tin roof until Joss had arrived safely back in Didja after their house-calls. He'd come instantly to the hospital to check on Gemma, where Melissa had taken great pleasure in announcing the results of their patient's tests. Afterwards he'd disappeared into his apartment, and she hadn't seen him until the next day.

Neither had mentioned the kiss, even though the attraction they were working hard at ignoring was still definitely palpable between them. But they both had things to do and concentrate on, and that was exactly what they were doing.

Even yesterday, when Joss had given Melissa her medical check-up, he'd been the consummate professional. Bub had been present as he'd checked her blood pressure, listened to her chest, checked her eyes and taken a blood sample.

'It's all just for insurance purposes,' he'd explained, before beginning.

'I completely understand. Standard procedure when starting a new job in a medical environment,' she'd replied, very aware that Bub was watching them very closely, no doubt picking up on the undercurrents which both doctors were working overtime at ignoring.

On the Friday two weeks after she'd been out on the house-calls with Joss—two weeks since he'd held her in his arms and kissed her so passionately—Melissa finished off her clinic and headed to her apartment.

She didn't feel like going to the pub this evening. She knew Dex was going, but during her time here he'd been merely polite and professional, treating her like just another colleague and nothing more. She knew she shouldn't feel hurt, but she did, and she couldn't face going to the pub and having her brother ignore her yet again.

But that's not the real reason, she told herself as she quickly did her dinner dishes and poured herself a relaxing glass of wine. She closed her eyes and gripped the kitchen counter with both hands as she admitted the real reason she didn't feel like company tonight—because Joss had been out all day on house-calls and he still wasn't back yet.

Of course Dex had initially been meant to go, and when she'd learned that Joss was doing them again she wondered whether he'd volunteered this time around. Perhaps it was simply easier for him to leave the clinic for a day and therefore not have to worry about running into her.

When she'd paid a quick visit to the hospital before leaving for the day, Bub had tut-tutted about 'poor Joss'.

'He's not what he used to be. There's something wrong with him. I can feel it.'

'Do you think he's sick?' Melissa asked.

'Not sick, but—oh, I don't know. Out of sorts, I guess is the best way to describe him. He snapped at Areva last Monday, and he's only been going to the pub on occasional nights. Incidentally,' she said, eyeing Melissa closely, 'he's been going on the nights that you *don't*. What is this? Tag team socialising? Only one of you can go at a time?'

'I think you'll find that Dex is usually there, so if Carto and Bluey decide to have another scrap there's at least one doctor on hand.'

'That's not what I'm talking about and you know it.' Bub sighed and lowered her tone. 'There's something going on between you and Joss.'

'No, there isn't.'

'OK. Let me rephrase that. There *should* be something going on between you and Joss. Even a blind man can see that you're both—'

'Don't say it.' Melissa held up her hand.

'He's a colleague. Nothing more. Dex is my brother. Nothing more.' She tried not to choke on the words as she said them. 'I'm learning to deal with those two facts, and right now I don't particularly want to talk about it, if you don't mind.'

Bub could see the strain on Melissa's face and smiled in acquiescence. 'Of course, darl. Go. Rest. Things will settle down eventually. You'll see.'

'I hope so, Bub.' And so she'd left, and decided that for tonight relaxing in her apartment was a definite must. There was a nice cool breeze, and Melissa decided to sit outside to try and unwind. At the rear of their apartments was a communal courtyard, and she carried her wine glass out through the back door towards the outdoor setting. It was quiet and peaceful, and she placed her glass on the table and sat, sighing heavily as she looked up at the stars.

'They're much brighter in the Outback, don't you think?' Joss spoke from just behind her, and Melissa jumped at the sound of his voice. 'Sorry. Didn't mean to scare you.' He walked over and sat in the chair opposite her.

'You're back!'

'No. Actually, this is a holographic image I had made up weeks ago, designed to keep people away from my relaxing courtyard.'

'*Your* relaxing courtyard?'

'Dex rarely comes out here.'

'So you've had it all to yourself for quite some time, then?'

'I have, but…' he pondered for a moment '… I guess I can share.'

'Does that mean the holographic projection is about to end?'

Joss grinned at her, loving that they were on the same wavelength. She understood him. It was just one more thing that helped fuel the attraction he felt for her. They might not have spoken much in the past two weeks, they might have been playing a slight avoidance game with each other, but it hadn't helped to change the way he thought about her—which was constantly.

He felt as though he was going around in circles and living in a perpetual state of confusion. Melissa was his colleague. She'd be here for quite some time. Tonight, instead of keeping his distance from her, he'd decided to seek her out and to hopefully try and come to a better arrangement than the avoidance one they were currently operating under. He had no idea what that arrangement might be, but it had to be better than where they both were at present.

'Hopefully not,' he replied.

'So…how were house-calls?'

'Good. Fine. Quite boring compared to the week we went out, actually. No emergencies. No pregnant women. No rampaging bulls.'

'Do you mean to tell me that isn't the usual way things run?'

He chuckled, and she allowed the sound to wash over her. He was definitely in a good mood and she wasn't about to ignore that fact.

'Today was lots of immunisations. Check-ups. That sort of thing.'

'The usual?'

'Basically, yes. How about you? Anything exciting happen in today's clinic?'

Melissa thought for a second, mainly because she couldn't get over how jittery she felt having him there, talking to her. She'd missed him, she realised. Missed just sitting and talking as they had out on Gemma's verandah. But, whilst she was delighted he'd sought her out, she was still a little wary at why he had. Did he have something drastic he needed to impart? Was he simply trying to be nice? She'd just have to go along for the ride and see where it ended up.

'Andy and James came in for their check-ups.'

'Good to hear. Rich is a stickler for follow-up appointments. A lot of bosses don't let their jackaroos have time off for follow-ups.'

'Well, they were both here and are generally doing fine. James had popped a few stitches. Thankfully Mindy had come to the rescue with her expert bandaging, so there was no infection. I've sorted him out now.'

'How did he pop his sutures?'

'He was horse riding.'

Joss shook his head. 'He would have been in trouble for that.'

'Yes. He said that Rich tore strips off him.'

'He's a good boss. Firm. Has his head screwed on, does Rich.'

'So you've said.'

'Sorry. Didn't mean to sound like a broken record.'

'You don't.'

'And how have things been going with Dex?'

Melissa shrugged. 'He's polite and all, but that's about it.'

'He's very slow. Takes a lot of time to process things.'

'You've said that before as well. I'm starting to wonder whether it wasn't a mistake, coming here.'

Joss felt as though she'd slapped him. He'd sought her out tonight in order to try and figure out a different way to deal with the attraction they felt. He'd hoped she was on the same page as him, wanting to move forward rather than to go around and around in circles, and now she was talking about leaving? He was stunned. 'You want to leave?'

'I don't know.' She shook her head and looked up at the stars. 'I don't know what I want any more. I'm confused.'

'Well, you can't leave,' he bristled, still a little shocked to have heard her speak that way. Just as well he hadn't come right out and confessed how she made him feel, because that would have been sacrificing himself yet again. 'Aren't you happy here?'

Melissa laughed without humour. 'Joss, since

I arrived my sedate, calm little life has been turned upside down and inside out.'

'Dex will come around.'

'I'm sure he will—but the question remains, do I need to be *here* when he does? I mean, I could leave, go work in Perth, write e-mails to him. When he's finished processing, when he's finished figuring things out, he could call me and then we could catch up. We wouldn't be living in each other's pockets.'

'But you have a contract,' he felt compelled to point out. He needed to stop all this talk of her leaving. She wasn't leaving. She *couldn't* leave. He needed her. Both for the clinic and for himself. However, there was no way he could tell her that. Not now.

'I know, Joss. Relax. I'm just thinking out loud.'

'So you're not happy here? Is that what you're saying?'

'Remember when I told you I was trying to like myself, to figure out who I really am? Well, I'm still trying to do that—but between you and Dex the confusion side of things reigns quite high.'

He sat up a little straighter in his seat. 'You're confused about me?'

Melissa laughed again and shook her head. 'What rock have you been living under?'

'Oh.' A dawning realisation crossed his face. '*That* type of confusion. Yeah, well, I'm right there alongside you when it comes to *that* type of confusion. We've both come from prior relationships that didn't work out, and in my case things not only didn't work out, I was completely betrayed. It's difficult to recover from something like that.' He took a deep breath. Maybe this was a good time to open up to her a little. He knew he needed to do it, and now was the perfect moment. 'When we were with the Etheringtons I found it really easy to talk to you.'

'Really?'

'Yes. Some of the things you said—such as liking yourself and being able to forgive your birth mother—really hit home. So I guess it might be time for me to open up a little, to tell you more about myself. But this isn't an easy thing for me to do.'

'Are you sure you *want* to do it?'

If there was ever going to be anything real between them then Joss needed to tell Melissa about his past. About *all* of it. It would also be a test to see how exactly she would react to what he was about to say.

'I am.'

'OK. I'm all yours…er…I mean I'm ready to listen, Joss.'

'Right.' He took a few deep breaths before plunging in. 'My fiancée, Christina, literally changed overnight, and I found myself facing a total stranger. I had no idea she was so deceptive, so dishonest, but apparently when things didn't turn out the way she planned she decided jumping ship was a far easier option than trying to understand.'

'Joss.' She could feel how painful this was for him. 'What on earth happened to make her not understand?'

'I was accused of medical negligence.'

Melissa gasped in horror. 'What?'

'It went to trial.'

'Oh, Joss.' She clutched her hands together to try and quell her anxiety.

'The patient who died was a man pretty high up in political circles so it was big news. The hospital offered me up as their sacrificial lamb.'

He had himself under control now and the

matter-of-fact way he spoke made her wonder just how often he'd gone over this story in his head to make it sound so emotionless. Surely he had to be hurting, had to have some feeling towards it?

'What a disgusting thing to do—although if it helps, I too have worked in hospitals that have corrupt administrators. They do exist.'

Joss nodded. 'I lost all faith. I wanted to quit medicine completely.'

'What stopped you?'

'Dex. My family. They stood by me. Supported me.'

'And Christina?'

He shook his head sadly. 'She joined the slander campaign, went to the media and painted me as some sort of monster. I was called "Doctor Death". Catchy, eh?'

Melissa's heart was bleeding for him and she wanted him to stop. To stop talking. To stop re-membering. To stop torturing himself.

She cared. Where Christina hadn't, Melissa did. She'd passed his silly test with flying colours, and his heart had started to open up once more. It was just the two of them, the moon and the stars, and he could see the glistening stream made from a lone tear which had slid silently down her cheek.

'Tears?'

'I can't believe what they did to you.' Emotion choked her words.

Joss leaned over and tenderly brushed the tear away with his thumb.

'You're a remarkable woman, Lis,' he whispered. 'Thank you.'

'For?'

'Listening. Believing. Caring. You are so incredibly beautiful. Do you know that? Do you have any idea just how much you affect me?' His words were soft as he came around the table to sit next to her. 'I can't help but watch you when you walk by. I find it difficult to concentrate when we're in business meetings simply because the scent of your perfume is driving me wild. I've hardly slept because I'm too busy lying awake, thinking of you on the other side of that wall. Imagining what you look like in your bed, lying beneath the whirring of the ceiling fan.'

She gasped at his words, unable to believe how closely his thoughts of her mirrored the ones she'd been having of him. 'Joss.' His name was a breathless whisper on her lips.

He swallowed. 'I like it when you wear your hair down, or just clipped back at the side as it is now. I like the way you relate to the patients. I like the way you listen so intently when someone is talking to you, focusing on them, making sure you don't miss a single syllable of what they're saying…just as you're doing now.'

Her breathing was shallow, her heart was pounding wildly beneath her chest and her body was alive with heat and wonder simply because of what he was saying. His words were like an aphrodisiac, and it was definitely working on her.

'I've missed you—and I'm not just talking about these past two weeks.' He shook his head as though to clear his thoughts. 'You've burst into my life. Until you came, I had no idea there *was* anything missing. You won't believe how many times I've wanted to just hold you, to drop a kiss to your lips, to see happiness light your eyes.'

Melissa could hardly breathe, but breathe she did as she met his gaze and urged him a little closer. 'Kiss me, Joss.'

The words were a whispered command and one he seemed more than ready to follow as he brought his mouth to meet hers for the first time in weeks.

She sighed as the touch, the taste and the hope she'd been dreaming about flowed freely through her body. It was a strange feeling to have a sense of belonging, but that was exactly how she felt every time Joss kissed her.

She loved the way his mouth seemed to fit perfectly to her own and her heart soared. He was remarkable as a man. He'd been through so much and yet he'd continued on with his life. He'd opened himself up to her, had shared a deep and intimate part of his past and trusted her with it. That spoke volumes.

'I feel so…alive,' she whispered against his mouth, her breathing erratic.

At her words, the heat between them intensified. Where he'd been a little concerned that he might scare her off, she matched him—moment for moment, sensation for sensation. The sweet sunshine of her scent became absorbed by his senses, fusing itself into his soul. Her soft moan of delighted pleasure became lodged in his memory, and he had a sense of deep satisfaction knowing that *he* was the person who had brought forth that sound from within her. He affected her just as much as she affected him. The taste of her mouth beneath his, the feel of her lips opening to his, accepting his need, became something he knew he'd crave for the rest of eternity.

'What do we do?' he choked out as he put his hands on her shoulders and drew them both apart. They stared at each other as rational thought slowly began to return.

'What do we do about…this?' she clarified, and he nodded.

'Yes. I mean, do we do anything about it at all? Do we go back to ignoring it?' Now that he'd told her about Christina, now that she'd passed his test and he'd seen just how sympathetic and understanding she really was, Joss wanted to know more about her. He wanted to spend more time with her. It was as though she'd managed to unlock a part of him he'd kept locked up for too long, and it made him wonder whether he really did have the strength to take that step and move forward with his life…take a step towards Melissa.

'Where will ignoring it get us?'

He thought for a moment. 'Back here, I guess. Fighting the attraction and then giving in to it.'

'Doesn't sound healthy.'

He eased back and raked a hand through his hair. 'This is so confusing.'

'Tell me about it.' Both of them thought for a moment. 'What about…going out on a date?' she suggested, not at all sure how he would respond.

'Dating?'

'Dinner, perhaps?' When he didn't say anything, she continued, 'Or not. I understand if you're reluctant.'

'It's not that. I'm more concerned about the fishbowl syndrome.'

'The community?' She raised her eyebrows. 'I guess I hadn't thought about it from that angle.'

'We're such a small, close-knit community. Everyone's bound to talk. We'll be the main discussion topic at every shop counter, at the bar in the pub, at the traffic lights in the street.'

'We can try keeping it quiet if you prefer, though I'm not sure how easy that will be. Joss, you've been the centre of attention in the past. Are you sure this is what you want?'

He shook his head. 'What I want is honesty,

Lis. If we're going to go out to dinner, then it needs to be done the right way. People will talk, but I guess…we'll get used to it.'

'So, dinner?'

'Yes.'

'When?'

He thought for a moment. 'How about tomorrow night? Saturday night is still date night, even out here in the middle of nowhere.'

She gulped. 'That soon? Boy, when you decide to move, you move!'

Joss grinned. 'I guess I do.'

'And do you have any thoughts on where we'll be having this date?' She hoped he didn't just take her to the pub, because that wouldn't feel like a date at all.

'Relax. I know just the place. Leave it to me.'

Later that night—after Joss had joined her in a glass of wine, after he'd walked her to her door and raised her hand to his lips in a gallant good-night kiss—Melissa stared up at the ceiling fan whirring above her bed, trying not to think of him on the other side of the wall.

Joss. The man she was sure she was falling in love with. The more he opened up to her, the more she liked him. Still she was racked with indecision, trying to figure out if she was really doing the right thing. Yes, she was almost positive she loved this man. Yes, she wanted to date him, to get to know him, to make this relationship work. But she'd had little success with relationships in the past because she'd been trying to use them to fill the empty void in her heart.

'But Joss is different,' she whispered. He made her feel one hundred percent alive whenever he listened to her, whenever he held her, whenever he kissed her. She was also concerned about Dex and his reaction to this turn of events.

Would this wreck her chances with Dex? Would this put even more distance between them? They were already estranged, and she didn't want that chasm to become any wider that it already was. Dex meant everything to her and the last thing she wanted to do was to hurt him.

Was going out with Joss—in front of the whole town—the right thing to do? She honestly had no idea.

CHAPTER TEN

As THEY walked side by side to the only really decent restaurant in town, Melissa was acutely aware of people looking at them. Everyone they passed called a greeting—'Hi, Docs.' Or, 'Nice night.' Or the typically Aussie greeting of 'How's it going?'

'I feel like everyone is looking at us,' she murmured as they continued along the footpath.

'That's because they are.' He'd known this would happen. He'd known going out on a date with Melissa would mean extra attention from the community. However, he was the one who'd insisted they keep whatever was happening between them as open and as honest as possible, so he'd just have to put up with the choking feeling which was telling him to run and hide.

'But we've walked down here together a few times and no one's paid us the slightest bit of attention,' she protested. 'We're not dressed any differently.' She motioned to their casual attire.

Joss looked at her and noted that she did look especially beautiful tonight. She was wearing a pair of three-quarter-length denims, a pale pink top and a simple gold chain. Her hair was loose, the way he liked it, and he shoved his hands into the pockets of his jeans to stop himself from sifting his fingers through her glorious locks.

When someone else called a friendly greeting to both of them, she felt as though a sign was pinned to her back. 'We're not even touching,' she pointed out.

'Yet I still feel as though everyone knows we're out on a date,' Joss confirmed as they walked past the pub.

'Hey, Joss!'

They both turned to see Carto and Bluey, waving at them with silly grins on their faces. 'How'd you get to be the lucky one taking the sheila doc out?' Bluey called.

Melissa closed her eyes for a split second, unable to believe this was happening. She didn't like being the centre of attention, but it appeared if she was going to date the gorgeous bachelor doctor, then she'd best get used to it. She smiled at the two larrikins.

'Probably because I shower regularly and wear deodorant,' Joss answered back, and with that he reached out and took Melissa's hand in his and continued up the street towards Stiggies. 'We may as well flaunt it,' he told her. 'Everyone already appears to know we're on a date.'

'I guess.' Melissa tried to cope with the mass of tingles which flooded her body at his touch. Joss was holding her hand—willingly holding her hand—in public! This man was such an enigma, and she was starting to wonder whether she shouldn't bother trying to figure him out but just go with whatever happened. He'd gone from swinging between hot and cold to being hot, hot, *hot*. Not that she was complaining, but after he'd told her about his past it had been as though he was a different person.

Perhaps telling her had removed a huge weight from him and given him the impetus he needed to move forward into the future? Or perhaps her reaction to the news had been some sort of test…one she'd obviously passed. He was very relaxed, very open, and he was holding her hand as they walked down the main street of Didja!

Melissa felt so self-conscious, still trying to figure out how everyone seemed to know they were on a date. As they walked into Stiggies, the owner himself came up to them. Stig was a short Italian man who had lived in Didja for most of his life yet still spoke with a strong Italian accent.

'Good evening, you two lovebirds. And how are you both this evening?'

Melissa and Joss looked at each other, then back to Stig. 'We're fine,' they replied in unison.

'Ahh…cute. I have your reserved table ready. Right this way.' Melissa let go of Joss's hand as Stig led them over to a candle-lit table in the most secluded corner of his establishment. The other patrons all called out greetings as they passed, everyone wearing silly goofy grins.

'You made a reservation?' Melissa whispered to Joss as they smiled their way through the restaurant. She felt like royalty, and wondered whether she shouldn't give a wave or two.

'Well, it's what you do when you have a date. I didn't want to turn up tonight and not be able to get a table. It is date night after all.'

They were seated and had assured Stig the table was perfect before being left alone to peruse the menu.

'How long has it been since you last reserved a table here?' she asked as she opened the menu but didn't even glance at it.

'Here? Uh…never.'

'You've never reserved a table before tonight?'

'No.'

'Then *that's* how everyone knows.' She closed her eyes and shook her head. So much for a quiet get-to-know-you evening. With everyone watching them it was going to be nigh on impossible to relax.

Joss shook his head slowly, clearly astounded. 'The news must have spread faster than a bushfire on a forty-two-degree day with a strong headwind.'

'Mystery solved.' Though she was still a little surprised at the *amount* of attention they were receiving.

'I didn't think when I made the reservation that it would receive such a reaction.' He looked around at the other patrons and saw they were all watching himself and Melissa quite closely. 'I feel like I really am living in a fishbowl.'

'Well, we did presume it would happen. People were bound to take an interest,' she pointed out. 'After all, you are quite the eligible bachelor, and they've never really seen you out on a date. It's big news. I wouldn't be surprised if we make the front page of the *Didja Gazette*.'

'I knew we'd be news, but I had hoped that for tonight we could…' He glanced around him again and smiled politely at all the other patrons who were watching them. 'Could have had a little privacy.'

'True, but…' Melissa put her menu down and looked at Joss. 'As that's not the case, we should simply forget everyone else and enjoy ourselves.'

Joss nodded. 'Agreed. We're out on our first official date, which is a big enough deal in itself, and we're going to enjoy ourselves.' He wanted very much to lean across the table and kiss her, to thank her for being so understanding in this town of eccentrics he'd chosen to live in, but he could still feel half the restaurant watching them so decided against it.

Their date continued, and after Stig had personally come to take their order, they chatted about their day.

'Excuse me.' Joss and Melissa looked up to find Bub standing beside their table. 'I'd like to say how wonderful it is to see you finally out with a beautiful woman, Joss.' She looked pointedly at Melissa. 'You're like a breath of sunshine to this town, darl, and I really hope everything works out for you.' Once that was said, she left.

Halfway through their entreés, Mr and Mrs Bloffwith came over and passed on their congratulations as well. Areva, the clinic receptionist, who was out on a date of her own, gave them the thumbs-up sign from across the room. Stig grinned widely at them both each time he brought them another course or refilled their wine glasses.

'We're thinking of booking the church for Valentine's Day,' said Veronica, the secretary out at the mine, when she came over to their table as they started on their desserts.

'Oh? What for?' Joss asked, totally perplexed.

Veronica laughed. 'For your wedding, of course.'

Melissa and Joss stared at each other in shock as Veronica headed off.

'Time to go?' Joss asked, feeling his breathing start to constrict.

'Time to go,' Melissa agreed. 'Desserts are seriously overrated.'

'Agreed.' He took Melissa's hand in his and headed towards the door, but not before calling over his shoulder, 'Thank you for a terrific meal, Stig. I'll settle up the account tomorrow.'

'Ahh…Dr Joss. This one is on the house, mate—after all, you've provided excellent dinner theatre for all my patrons tonight.'

'Thanks. So glad we could oblige,' Joss remarked as he held the door for Melissa. 'Goodnight, all.'

'Night,' everyone chorused, and as they exited Melissa couldn't help but let go of the giggle which had been bubbling up all night long.

She looked around, noting there were fewer people out and about now.

'I'd just like to say, Dr Lawson, that you definitely know how to show a girl a memorable first date.'

Joss grinned. 'I do, don't I?' He gave her hand a little squeeze. 'Talk about life imitating a sitcom.'

'Oh, I don't know that it was. The setting was very romantic, the food was divine and the company was first class.'

Joss was pleased with her words. When he'd

realised the whole town was watching them, he'd been interested to see how she would handle the attention—and she'd done a mighty fine job. She hadn't thrown a tantrum, hadn't demanded he take her home as he'd half expected. Then again, he had to keep reminding himself that Melissa wasn't like other women—and particularly wasn't like Christina.

He looked at her and she smiled up at him. He couldn't resist the allure of her mouth any longer and leaned down to brush a light kiss across her lips. 'Thank you.'

'For?'

'For being you.'

'Oh, well, I'm good at that. I've had plenty of practice.'

He smiled at her words. 'Seriously, Lis, I don't think you realise just how much you've helped me.' Joss shook his head. 'I never thought I'd go out on a date. I never thought I'd be able to let go of my past, take a step forward and actually try dating again.' He stopped walking for a moment, pulling her into his arms. 'Just having you here, listening to me, taking an interest in me, it really has helped.'

'I'm glad.' His words were heartfelt, and she appreciated how difficult it must have been for him to say them, but at the back of her mind Melissa wondered whether she hadn't just slipped into her people-pleasing role in order to help Joss get over his past. Had she? Had she put him before herself? It was what she'd done with Renulf. It was what she'd done all her life. She didn't want to start another possible relationship being the one who always made the compromises.

She was certain now, as she looked up into his eyes in the dim evening light, that she loved him. She loved Joss, and it was a deeper, more abiding love than she'd felt before, but surely that meant she should be extra-cautious? She'd given her heart before and had it broken. Could she risk it again? Sure, he was grateful for the help she'd given him—but how did he *feel* about her? Did he feel more than gratitude? Did he simply see her as someone who would be working here in the clinic and helping him out with his problems?

Joss tightened his arms around her and she smiled up at him, pushing her thoughts aside. 'I'm glad you came to Didja,' he remarked, and he started to lower his head.

The kiss wasn't as dynamic as the one they'd shared in the ute, it wasn't as hot or as heavy, and although it was still delightful she couldn't help but think he was holding a lot of himself back.

Someone outside the pub wolf-whistled at them and they quickly broke apart.

'Get her to agree to the kissing booth!' a bloke called.

'Rack off, Bluey,' Joss remarked, then looked down at Melissa. 'Sorry about that.' He shook his head.

'Am I going to be bugged about a kissing booth for the rest of my life?'

He chuckled. 'Probably—but I promise that if you ever decide to hold a kissing booth I shall be the one buying up every single kiss.'

She sighed and tightened her arm around him. 'My hero.' As they continued on past the pub Melissa looked in and saw Dex standing at the bar, talking to yet another pretty blonde.

'He's at it again.' Joss rolled his eyes.

'He's definitely quite the charmer—or so I've been told.'

'I'm looking forward to the day when some woman waltzes into town and knocks him for six.'

Melissa laughed and nodded. 'I think I'd like to be around for that show as well.' They continued down the street, Joss's arm still close around her.

'Poor Dex. He was like a bear with a sore head when he first discovered he was adopted.'

'What do you mean? First discovered? You mean he was angry when I initially tried to make contact?'

'Yes. Until that time Dex had no idea he was adopted. He has two younger siblings—siblings he thought were his real brother and sister.'

Melissa's eyes widened in total shock. 'I don't believe it! His parents never told him?' Her tone was one of utter incredulity.

'No. It was a really difficult time for him, but he got through it.'

'No wonder he didn't want to see me back then. And that's why he's been so reticent since.' She shook her head slowly. Why hadn't someone told her earlier? 'I had no idea.'

'He needs time to process everything. That's all. It's what we guys do.'

'Go into your caves? Hide yourselves away?'

'Something like that.'

'Is that in the hope that the problem might

simply go away, or so you can figure out a solution to it?'

'Both—but mostly the latter.'

'And there's no telling how long these cave-dwelling activities can go on for?'

Joss shrugged. 'Depends on the man, depends on the problem, and depends on whether or not he has cable TV in the cave.'

She chuckled and shook her head. 'Men!' They were standing outside her apartment now and he pulled her into his arms, drawing her close. Melissa's arms went around his neck.

'We're an interesting species,' he confirmed.

'I can think of a few other adjectives,' she said, and he laughed.

'I'm sure you can, but right now I don't want you to think.' And he lowered his head, capturing her lips with such delicacy that all thought fled to be replaced by delighted tingles.

Two days later, with the town still gossiping about the dating doctors, Melissa found it difficult to focus on her clinic. She had a full schedule, and yet she kept falling behind as patient after patient grinned like a Cheshire cat and asked her all sorts of personal questions about her relationship with Joss.

She was never more glad when she was able to sneak into the kitchen for fifteen minutes to eat a bite of lunch. Joss soon walked in and sat down next to her.

'How's your morning been?'

'Exhausting,' she said.

'We're one hot topic.'

'You're not wrong. Hey, do you know where Dex is? I expected to see him around this morning.' She wanted to know what he thought about herself and Joss.

'He's gone out to the mine to do occupational health and safety checks. He volunteered, actually, even though I was rostered on. I think he wanted me to stay here and face the music.' Joss laughed.

'You know, Joss, I've been thinking that maybe we should take a few steps back for a while.'

'Why?'

Melissa shrugged. She'd been thinking about it since the other night, and was still uncertain of exactly how to explain to him what she was feeling. Joss was more than happy to hold her, to kiss her, to be seen in public with her—but she wanted more. She'd been in a relationship where only certain aspects had been satisfied and she didn't want to enter into another one.

If Joss was only attracted to her on a physical level, if he only needed her for his clinic, then she wasn't interested. She loved him, and it pained her to say what she was about to, but she'd made a promise to herself never to settle for anything but absolute perfection in a relationship, and at the moment she simply wasn't getting that.

'Why?' She sighed heavily. 'Good question. I guess I'm feeling a little disconcerted, a little disjointed. You know, things haven't really worked out the way I planned when I initially made the decision to come to Didja. I had no idea that Dex didn't know he was adopted, and it makes me realise that he needs a lot more space then he's getting. Me being here is a constant reminder of that, and it can't be easy for him to deal with.'

Joss eased back in his chair, nodding slowly. 'You're thinking about leaving?'

Melissa closed her eyes for a moment, trying to say the words she needed to say but not wanting to hurt him at the same time. It was then she realised that if she didn't say what was on her heart she'd risk hurting herself a lot more. Looking at him again, she swallowed. 'There's a great attraction between us, Joss. Has been from the first moment we saw each other. We've both tried to fight it and it didn't work; it only became stronger. I'm glad I was able to help you move through your pain about Christina, and I can't thank you enough for trusting me with such intimate knowledge…'

'But…?' He folded his arms over his chest.

'But I don't know if I've sorted through my own past. I've told you I was in a relationship where things didn't quite gel. I've put myself second in every relationship I've had, and now I'm doing it again with both you and Dex. I don't know if I'm strong enough to survive another rejection.'

'So you're rejecting me first?'

'I'm not rejecting you. I'm trying to protect myself.'

'What are you saying? You want to leave?'

'Can you give me a reason why I should stay?' Her eyes were imploring. She knew he was attracted to her, she knew he liked talking to her, but what she was looking for was a stronger commitment. She loved him, and she needed to be loved in return. Was it too soon? Would he be able to give her what she needed?

'You're contracted until the end of the year.'

'Anything else?'

'What about Dex? He does need you, Melissa. More than you know. You're the only one who can help him through what he's going through. You're the only one who really understands.'

There was a veiled hint of urgency in his tone. He'd just stepped forward into the light. He'd finally been able to leave the past where it needed to be and move into the future…a future he wanted with her. She was amazing. She was sexy. She was intelligent. He was sure he was on the way to falling in love with her. Never had he met a woman so incredible, so determined and so gutsy. She'd put up with him in all states of confusion, and he was grateful she hadn't let him push her away.

'I don't need to be in Didja to help Dex.'

'You have a gift for getting people to open up. To talk out their problems. You're so great with the patients. This community needs you.'

'They need a female doctor. That doesn't necessarily mean they need *me*.' She shrugged.

Joss stood from his chair, almost knocking it to the ground with utter frustration. He raked a hand through his hair, his agitation increasing. 'What do you want from me? The town needs you.'

'And?' Her tone was urgent.

'And Dex needs you.'

'And?' Melissa's tone was almost pleading.

'And I—' He stopped. Could he do this? Could he confess to her how he really felt?

'And what, Joss? *What?*' Hope was surging wildly through her. Could it be that he felt more for her than she'd realised? 'What?' she pleaded again.

Joss swallowed. 'I—'

'Joss! Joss!' Areva came running into the kitchen. 'There's been a bad accident at the mine. They've just called it through.'

Joss frowned. 'Dex's out there. Isn't he there? Can't he handle it?'

'That's just it. You don't understand. Dex *is* the emergency.'

'What?' Both Melissa and Joss spoke in unison.

Joss looked over at Melissa and saw the blood drain from her face.

'Is he all right? What happened?' She was starting to shake, to hyperventilate, and Joss immediately pushed her head between her knees.

'Breathe. Relax.' His voice was quiet and reassuring. Melissa focused on it, needing his soothing, sultry tones to calm her. He looked to Areva. 'What's the information?'

'Veronica called through to say there had been an accident in the workshop. Dex left his ute at the mine workshop because the guys there said they'd do an oil change for him, and when Dex was finished he went back to collect it. That's when the accident happened. He got hurt because of some tyre thing exploding.' Areva's words were disjointed as she stumbled over what Veronica had reported.

'Right. Areva, I need you to let Bub know what's happened, so she can organise the operating theatre and call in whatever staff she needs. Also, if you wouldn't mind cancelling the rest of our clinics, that would be great.'

'Oh. Right. Sure.' Areva headed off and Joss turned his full attention to Melissa, who was slowly sitting up.

'How are you feeling?'

'OK. A little dizzy, but OK.'

He had one hand on her arm, the other around her shoulders as he looked intently at her.

'You have a little more colour. Just breathe deeply.'

'We need to go and get Dex.' Urgency and panic laced her voice within her tone.

'And we will. But I need to know that you'll be all right to handle whatever we find. I'm sure Dex isn't too badly hurt, but even if he is we'll help him. We're his friends as well as his family. Trust me, Lis. Dex is just like another brother to me, and if there's one thing I do and do well it's look after my own.' He stood, holding out a hand to help her to her feet. 'Are you with me?'

Melissa took one last deep breath in and let it slowly out. The dizziness had settled. The panic was under control. Her brother—her only living relative—needed her now more than ever. With Joss, she would help Dex. They would be there for him. The two of them. Strong enough to pull him through whatever faced him. They would do this, and they were going to do it together. She placed her hand in his and slowly rose to her feet.

'I'm ready.'

He'd watched as she'd mentally pulled herself together, marvelling at how incredible this woman was. She'd faced so many hardships in her life, and it was her strength which continued to get her through. He honestly felt her pain because he'd meant what he'd said—Dex *was* like another sibling to him—but what they needed most right now was to keep level-headed if they were going to be able to get Dex through.

His eyes were alight with pride. 'You're a strong woman, Melissa Clarkson. I love that about you.' He gave her hand a little squeeze. 'Let's get to work.'

They both packed medical bags, Joss making sure the emergency kit was fully stocked. As they hadn't yet received a more detailed report on specific injuries they were flying blind. They had saline and plasma, IV lines, morphine, bandages, neck braces and much more.

'Do you want to go and quickly change?' he asked as he packed everything into his ute. 'Your clothes will get dirty at the mine.'

She looked down at her navy trousers and red knit top. She didn't care. They were just clothes. Getting to Dex was more important than what she was wearing. 'I'm fine. Why don't we have an ambulance?'

'What use is an ambulance when I have the ute? The suspension is better than any ambulance, because as a general rule ambulances aren't four-wheel drive. I have a firm mattress in the tray, blankets and rope—all perfect for transferring patients short distances.' He looked across at her and then shook his head. 'We do need one. I've applied for funding, but…unless the town gets bigger…'

'Which it will. We have so many pregnant women at the moment.' She climbed into the ute and looked across at him as they put on their seat-belts. Putting a hand on his shoulder, she nodded warmly. 'You'll get your ambulance, Joss. You're an amazing man who has provided an incredibly high level of medical care for this community. You give and you give and you keep on giving. What a big heart you have, Josiah Lawson.' She smiled at him and caressed his cheek. 'I love that about you.'

It was probably the nicest thing anyone had ever said to him, and sincerity was there in her eyes. She was quite a woman.

'Dex…' he murmured, and she dropped her hand back to her side.

'Let's go help our brother.'

When they arrived at the mine site they were met at the gate by Jeff.

'Follow me. I'll take you to the workshop. Switch your UHF to six.' He walked ahead of them and climbed into his own ute. He drove down a large gravel road, leading the way further down into the enormous open cut mine. Even though Melissa was concerned for Dex, even though she was running through possible scenarios in her mind, she still couldn't help being overwhelmed at the sheer size of everything.

The enormous dump trucks that made trips up and down the slopes all day long, hauling their loads, were like something from Giant Land. The wheels themselves were as tall as a house, the drivers needing to climb a ladder just to get into them.

'You there?' Jeff's voice came over the UHF radio and Joss quickly lifted the handset and answered.

'Go ahead.' He replaced the handset and they both listened.

'Dex is still in the workshop. We have two other men involved. They were fixing dual wheels, removing the outside one, when the energy in the inner tyre was violently released. One man is dead, the other critically injured. Dex was there, too. He was thrown back quite fiercely. I've been down to see the area and I have informed head office in Perth.'

Melissa grabbed the handset and tried to talk into it, but nothing happened.

'Press the button,' Joss instructed.

'Oh.' She did so. 'What about Dex? When you saw him, was he OK?'

'He was up. He confirmed Milko's death. He was treating Vitchy when I left.'

'He's really OK?' Melissa couldn't believe the relief which coursed through her, and she sagged back against the seat.

'I don't know. He looked it. He has a few cuts and stuff. Here we are. Now, wait until I give the all-clear for you to get out of the car. OK?' Jeff's tone was stern. There had already been one fatality today, and he wasn't taking any chances on anything else going wrong.

Jeff walked around, checking everything out, and Melissa thought her impatience was going to burst through the roof. Dex was inside the workshop. They were parked outside the workshop. So near, yet so far.

'Relax.' Joss put a hand on her knee. 'I need you focused, remember? Deep breaths.'

'Deep breaths. Right.' She closed her eyes for a moment and concentrated. 'Right. Focused.'

'That's it.' Joss watched her, unable to believe how incredibly beautiful she was. Did she have any idea? He felt her pain and he wanted to help in any way he could. He wanted to be there for her, to support her, to let her know she *wasn't* all alone in this world.

He loved her. He still couldn't believe it himself, but it was the truth—and it was a truth he wanted to shout to the world. Finally he'd been able to shrug off his past, to step into the future, and it was a future he wanted to spend with her. He loved her and he didn't care who knew it! Being able to be here for her, to support her in a time of crisis, had helped him to realise the most powerful truth in the world—he loved her with all his heart.

For now, though, they needed to put their personal relationship aside and focus on this emergency. There would be time enough for declarations and plans later on.

Jeff knocked on the ute's window and both of them nearly jumped out of their skins. 'Ready,' Jeff called, and with a calm eagerness Joss and Melissa exited the cabin, collected their medical kits from the back and followed Jeff inside.

She hadn't been at all sure what to expect, but the sight of one of the enormous trucks startled her for a second. The 'workshop', as Jeff had called it, was more like an aeroplane hangar—it had to be to fit the dump trucks inside. It was just so enormous, and seeing one of the trucks up close, as opposed to driving around in the quarry, was quite overwhelming.

'Around here,' Jeff directed, and they carefully walked around the truck to the other side. The scene that met them there was one of total chaos. The explosion of the tyre had been so violent that the windows had shattered, tools and equipment had been blasted off shelves and debris littered the entire section.

Dex was half-sitting, half-reclining in the mess. He was lying next to a man she presumed was Vitchy, as the supine worker had a bandage around his arm and a pressure pad to his eye. Melissa rushed over to Dex, putting her medical kit down beside him.

'Took your time,' he muttered.

'Well, you were a little difficult to find,' Joss responded, coming to the other side of Vitchy. 'What's the diagnosis?'

'Fractured right arm, fractured tibia, vision impaired.' Dex stopped, his breathing heavy and laboured. 'Uh…' He closed his eyes to think, and Melissa immediately put her hand to his wrist, checking his pulse. His eyes snapped open at her touch. 'I'm fine. You need to deal with Vitchy. Milko's gone. He was too close to the tyre. It exploded. Shrapnel ripped through him.'

Melissa kept her thoughts focused. 'Dex, your pulse is weak. Did you hit your head? Get thrown back?' She was reaching for her stethoscope as she asked the questions.

'I'm fine.'

'Answer her,' Joss ordered as he performed his own observations on Vitchy.

'You always were bossy in an emergency.' Dex tried to make light of the situation, but as he forced a laugh he groaned in pain.

'Where does it hurt?'

'I'm still mad at you,' he murmured, looking up at Melissa. 'My life was mine before you came into it. You...ruptured it.'

'Understood,' she said, acknowledging what he was saying. She couldn't pretend his words didn't hurt her, but at least he was saying them out loud. At least he was really communicating with her for the first time. 'Now, tell me, where does it hurt?'

'Hurts to breathe. Lots of lower abdominal pain.'

She listened to his chest. 'You may have a small puncture to your lung.' She then listened to his abdomen, moving the instrument around, listening carefully. 'I can't tell. I'll need to ultrasound the area.'

'Well, at least I'm not pregnant, right?'

Melissa continued to check him. 'Not this time.'

'So I'll be fine. I'm just winded—and I think I might have eaten something bad at lunchtime. Wazza made cheese soufflé, and maybe the cheese part wasn't—*owww!*' He slapped at

Melissa's hand as she gently palpated his abdomen. 'That hurts, Lis.'

'Sorry.'

Joss looked at Melissa and met her gaze. Instinctively they both knew things weren't right with Dex, and the sooner they got him back to the hospital the better. Joss called Jeff over. 'Get another ute set up to take Vitchy to the hospital. We'll need help loading the patients into the vehicles. Make sure the coroner knows about Milko, and arrange—'

'I've just been informed that it's all been taken care of.' Jeff glanced across to where his deceased friend still lay, covered with a tarp. His jaw clenched, but he was a professional and he needed to behave as such.

Joss made a mental note to speak to the mine psychologist as Milko's friends and family would need counselling over this incident.

'Right. You'll find the items you need to set up the other ute in the tray of mine. There's a—'

'I know the drill.' Jeff turned and left the large workshop.

When Melissa checked Dex's blood pressure, it was to find it rather low. She set up a saline drip and gave him an injection of morphine.

'How is he?' Joss asked as they stood to one side, where Dex couldn't hear them.

'Not good. I think he has an internal bleed. The lung seems to be holding, but, Joss…' There was pain, panic and a penetrating urgency in her voice. 'We need to get him back to the hospital, *stat*.'

'Agreed. Vitchy will require surgery, but for now, thanks to Dex, he's stable.'

'How did he manage to care for Vitchy when he himself is so badly injured?'

'Adrenaline. We'll get him sorted out.' He placed a comforting arm around her shoulders, drawing her closer. The desire to protect her was now totally overwhelming. 'I promise you.'

Melissa looked up at him and saw the truth of his statement in his eyes. 'I believe you.'

And at that moment he realised she did. Not only did she believe him, he saw that she believed *in* him. She trusted him. He was struck with an incredible insight that if his world ever came crumbling down in a pile of rubble again, if she was the woman by his side she'd never desert him.

* * *

By the time Dex was back at the clinic his blood pressure was dropping quite rapidly, despite replacement fluids via an intravenous line.

'I can't wait for an ultrasound. I need to go in now, find the source of the bleed and get it clamped, *stat*.' Joss's tone was brisk.

Bub had everything organised, except for an anaesthetist. 'Dex usually does anaesthetics,' she pointed out to Joss.

'I'll do it,' Melissa volunteered. 'I've done it plenty of times.'

'You'll be all right?' Joss checked.

'I will. We need to focus and save his life. Now, do we need to cross type and match?'

Joss shook his head. 'No. Dex's blood type is the same as yours. Lis, there's something very special you can do for your brother, because we don't keep blood in stock. I've got him on plasma, but getting some replacement blood into him will give him that extra boost he needs.'

She held out her arm to Bub and tapped at her vein. 'Let's get this blood flowing. We've got my brother's life to save.'

* * *

Dex's surgery was long and meticulous. It was the first real opportunity Melissa had had to watch Joss operate, and she marvelled at how natural and brilliant he was at the task. He should be doing surgery full-time. He should be head of a surgical department. He should be lecturing, teaching others. Yet being here with him, in the Outback, caring for this community, she knew he was in exactly the right place at the right time.

The surgery progressed, and the nurses proved themselves to be well trained.

'Ahh. Finally—there it is. Offensive little artery,' he muttered, before clamping it off and continuing with the rest of the operation.

When it was time for her to reverse the anaesthetic, Dex's blood pressure was steadily increasing back into the normal range. She'd been able to give a unit of blood, which had really helped. Still, she would give him as much blood as he needed. He was her brother and she loved him.

'He's got a long recovery ahead of him,' Joss commented as they wheeled Dex to the ward.

When Bub had her star patient all settled, Joss

and Melissa stood at the end of his bed, watching him sleep.

'We'll be there for him. We'll get him through.'

Her words carried such determination and love that Joss was once again struck by her inner strength. He put his arm around Melissa's shoulders and she instantly snuggled into him, placing one hand on his chest and sighing. He realised this was more than just comforting her. This was him *being there* for her.

It was an important moment, and Melissa wondered whether Joss's feelings for her were far deeper than he was letting on. Could she hope? Should she stay? Would leaving Didja be the right or the wrong thing to do?

They stayed for quite some time, both of them content to simply be with each other, watching the man who was dear to both of them. Then Melissa gave another few units of blood whilst Joss went to check on Vitchy. When he was satisfied with Vitchy's condition he returned to Dex's bedside, watching him, Melissa still sitting there holding her brother's hand. Finally Bub kicked them out of the ward, telling them they were in her way as she went about looking after her patients.

'When are you planning to operate on Vitchy?' Melissa asked as they walked through the quiet clinic to their apartments.

'I'll review him tomorrow and go from there. Rushing into surgery too early will simply cause further complications. Besides, most of his injuries are orthopaedic, so once he's stable we'll need to transfer him to Perth.'

When they arrived at her apartment door Joss pulled her close, simply holding her. After a while, Melissa spoke softly.

'Before I came to Didja I don't think I really had a true sense of who I am, deep down inside. I think I never really gathered a sense of who I am because I'd always lose myself in every relationship. I was a daughter caring for elderly parents. Then I was caring for Eva. Then I attached myself to a man who had an abundance of family and a loving heart. But it still wasn't me. That was why I *had* to search Dex out.'

'A journey of self-discovery?' Joss had come to the conclusion that if she really wanted to leave Didja, if she needed some space, then he'd give it to her. He wouldn't like it, but he didn't want to pressure her into loving him.

'If you like.'

'And have you discovered anything?' He tried not to hold his breath. He tried not to wonder at what she might say.

'Quite a few things, actually.'

'Such as?'

'I love it here in Didja. I love the people, and you're right—they *are* like a family.'

'And you have Dex.'

'I hope so.'

'You do. Especially after today. He needs you, Lis.'

What about you? She wanted to ask the question, to really find out just how Joss felt about her, but she yawned as the events of the day, both physical and emotional, started to catch up with her.

'You're tired,' he murmured. 'You need to sleep.'

'Is that your way of telling me I look haggard?' She smiled up at him.

'It's my way of forcing myself to leave you to sleep.' He kissed the tip of her nose. 'Goodnight, my Lis. Sleep sweet.'

* * *

For the next few days Melissa visited Dex regularly, taking breaks between her patients to go and sit with him. He'd recovered well from surgery and was improving at a dramatic rate. On Thursday Joss came with her after clinic had finished, and she was glad to have him beside her. He'd proved himself time and time again to be interested in her, to be interested in how she was coping with Dex, and Melissa's love for him grew.

'I always heal quickly, too,' she told Dex. 'Something else we have in common.'

'Is there anything I can say to make either of you go away?' Dex asked.

'Nope.'

'So we have stubbornness in common as well.'

She smiled. 'Yes.' Melissa paused, then took a deep breath. 'Dex, if there's anything you want to know about our birth mother—about why she had you adopted, things like that—then all you need to do is ask.' She placed her hand over her heart. 'I had no idea you didn't know you were adopted. My parents told me from the get-go, but then again I was almost three years old when they adopted me.'

'What? I thought you were a baby?' Dex was stunned.

'No. I don't remember those first few years of my life, but from what our birth mother, Eva, told me, there were times when she could barely afford to feed us.'

Joss shook his head sadly. 'Must have been tough for her.'

'It was.'

'Is she the one who wanted you to hunt me down?'

'I'm not *hunting you down*, Dex. When you say it like that you make it sound so merciless. I simply want to get to know you.'

'Why? I think that's a fair question. *Why?*'

'Because I don't have anyone else. My adoptive parents were both very ill and died four years ago. Eva died not too long ago. I have no one else, Dex. No aunts, uncles, siblings, long-lost cousins. You...you are the only blood relative I have, and I need you.'

Dex stared at her from his hospital bed. 'You have no one?'

'No.'

'You have Joss.' He pointed to where the two of them sat side by side.

'He's not my brother.'

'And just as well,' Joss replied with a grin, taking Melissa's hand in his own.

He'd thought a lot over the last few days, and whilst she hadn't said anything else about wanting to leave Didja, he wanted to show her just how important she was to him. Not because of the clinic or the community but because of *him*.

'Actually.' Joss cleared his throat, deciding to take the bull by the horns and step way out of his comfort zone. It was important. Melissa was important. 'That's something I've been meaning to talk to you about. You see, I find myself with a bit of a dilemma.'

'What's that?' Dex asked.

'I need to ask you a question, Dex, and I'm not really sure what your answer's going to be.'

At his words, Melissa felt as though her heart had stopped beating and she looked up at him. He sounded so serious. She looked from one man to the other and back again.

Joss cleared his throat again, and looked at his friend. 'As you are Melissa's brother, and her only living relative, I feel it's only fitting that I ask your permission to marry her.'

'What?' Brother and sister spoke in unison, and behind them Bub dropped a dressing tray she was carrying towards the hospital bed.

Joss rubbed his chin with his free hand. 'Not really the reaction I'd been expecting.'

'You want to…to…?' Melissa couldn't finish the words and she simply stared up at him, her heart overflowing with love.

Joss looked intently into her eyes. 'To marry you? Yes. More than anything. First, though…' he tore his gaze away from Melissa's to look at Dex '…I need Dex's permission.'

'This really is serious.' Dex was astounded. 'I thought you were just joining the real world again. You know…dating and stuff. I didn't realise it was *love*.'

'And now that you realise it?'

Joss hadn't denied it. He hadn't denied that he loved her. Melissa was so glad she was sitting down, because otherwise she knew she'd have crumpled in a heap on the floor. Joss loved her! Could this really be happening? Was she about to awake from the best dream ever? She hoped not.

Dex looked to Melissa and then back to his

friend. 'Take her. Marry her. Make her happy.' He pointed a finger at his friend in warning. 'But just remember I have a pygmy blow-gun in my apartment and I'm not afraid to use it!'

Joss nodded, trying not to smile. 'In that case, you have my word that I will do my utmost to make her very happy.'

He turned to face Melissa, lowering himself to one knee. Holding both her hands, his tone clear and filled with conviction, as he started to speak.

'Melissa Clarkson, I love you. You've touched me deeply and helped me to let go of my past and start looking towards my future…the future I want to share with you. You wanted a definite reason to stay in Didja and I'm giving you one. I'm not trying to shackle you to me or to the clinic. I want you here because I love you with all of my heart. I need you by my side, to help me to continue to grow and so that I can also help you. We'll be equals—a complete loving partnership.'

The love was reflected in his eyes, in a look of pure sincerity, and she knew he meant everything he was saying. 'I need you, Lis, and I promise you won't be alone. Not any more. I want you to marry me and to fill our house with a loving family—which is what we both not only want but need in our lives. There's no one else I want to be the mother of my children except you, my lovely Lis.' He squeezed her hands and brushed a quick kiss across her lips. 'Please…' he implored. 'Will you do me the honour of becoming my wife?'

Melissa couldn't believe it. She couldn't believe this was happening. The man of her dreams was not only declaring his love for her, but was asking her to be with him for ever. He was also waiting for an answer.

'Joss.' She swallowed over her nervousness, projecting her voice, strong and true. 'I love you. I love you for so many different reasons. For accepting me. For supporting me. For saving my brother's life.' Tears started to gather in her eyes, but they were tears of pure happiness. 'But most of all I love you for who you are and for needing me in your life. You're an amazing man and I adore you.' She reached out and caressed his cheek, her eyes filled with love. 'I would be delighted to be your wife.'

Dex cheered, and Bub joined in, the two of them making so much noise it was almost as if they were in the pub!

Joss stood and swept Melissa up into his arms, planting a firm but sure kiss to her lips. 'You've made me so happy,' he said softly near her ear.

'The feeling is one hundred percent mutual.'

'No more talk of leaving Didja?'

'Why would I want to leave when everything I need in my life is right here?' Melissa kissed him again with all the passion and desire in her heart, and without a hint of doubt. He was the man for her, the most perfect man for her, and finally she felt as though she truly belonged.